Other Books in English
by Carlos Maleno

The Irish Sea

Carlos Maleno

THE ENDLESS ROSE

Translated by Eric Kurtzke

DALKEY ARCHIVE PRESS
Dallas / Dublin

Originally published in Spanish as *Mar de Irlanda* by Editorial Sloper, 2014

Copyright © 2015 by Carlos Maleno

Translation © 2023 by Eric Kurtzke

First edition

Paperback: 978-1-62897-317-4
Ebook: 978-1-62897-495-9

Library of Congress Cataloging-in-Publication Data: Available.

Cover design by Nuno Moreira
Interior design by Anuj Mathur

Dalkey Archive Press
www.dalkeyarchive.com
Dallas/Dublin

Printed on permanent/durable acid-free paper.

What are they gonna do when the lights go down
without you to guide them to Zion?

What are they gonna do when the rivers overrun other
than tremble incessantly?

And what am I to say to all these ghouls tonight?

—MAYNARD JAMES KEENAN

. . . our generation, our perspectives, our models of Fear.

—ROBERTO BOLAÑO

The desert has the best climate for violence.

—EDUARDO RUIZ SOSA

The Demiurge is a hermaphrodite.

—ALFRED KUBIN

The Endless Rose

DETECTIVES LOST IN THE BRIGHT CITY

1.

Who could deny that she was the one who enlightened him? At least during that part of his life. He rationalized her stories, threw bleach on their plots, until he found his way of life in them. Not one of you could deny this, none of you were there, not like she was. He searched for his shelter and sense in her arms, her darkness was his light. He learned to love her and she reciprocated. None of you could deny his romance with death.

She was the light and the way.

And it started with a sentence, this one:

It is possible to love only that which stands above us.

That was what Roberto Fate said to himself, late into the night, as he tossed a handful of papers on the coffee table, the manuscript by Paula Boccia, barely a hundred pages long. At first, as he leaned back on the old leather sofa in the dim light, a feeling of unreality came over him. Then he thought of that woman, of her writing,

that disappeared into itself—chaotic, brutal, savage, sui-
cidal—like automatic writing, or the writing of a lunatic.

Then, without caring about the late hour, he called the
phone number printed on the first page of the manuscript.
At the other end of the line, nobody answered.

Then the rain began to fall on Almería, and Roberto
Fate, who was thirty-seven years old and ran a publishing
house, stood gazing at his own reflection in the window-
pane, on the other side of which misty raindrops streamed
down, and pictured himself teetering over an abyss, as he
had repeatedly imagined over the last few months. Teetering
like a tightrope walker on the narrow wire made of his fond
hopes and love of literature. Teetering over the abyss of
uncertainty, the abyss where he could lose the money he'd
managed to scrape together in earlier days, days that now
seemed immeasurably distant; the abyss where he found
nothing, not finding the author he could wholeheartedly
bet on, where everything ended in ugliness and vanity,
or where the author was found, and all in vain. This last
possibility didn't really trouble him.

Then he considered the characters from that slim manuscript of stories he'd received, reluctantly at first—on the
house website, it was unpublished novels, between one
and two hundred pages, that they were soliciting—but
then with a feeling of pleasant surprise at encountering
something he hadn't expected.

It is possible to love only that which stands above us. So
began Paula Boccia's first story. In the story, a monkey, or
what appeared to be a monkey, talks about its life, about
its present and past, and it seemed to Roberto that what
he was reading was a children's story, until he realized that
the narrator wasn't a monkey but an abnormally hirsute

man who called himself Monkey, and gradually, as he read on, Roberto began to feel that some of the pieces didn't fit, and realized that this man wasn't a man, he was something else, and that, actually, none of the pieces fit, or at least not quite as they should, and then the story abruptly ended, and the narrator, who was no longer a monkey, who was no longer a man, who was something else, beset the reader with a terrible question. And being the reader he was, Roberto—a man or now perhaps not exactly—repeated the question to himself, and felt even stranger.

Then he went to the kitchen, reheated some black coffee, stirred in a teaspoon of sugar, and returned to the sofa, where he covered himself with a small blanket and got ready to read the manuscript a second time. Before focusing on his reading, he thought of the brief journey he'd taken down the hallway. He thought of the moments before he'd switched off the kitchen light, when he'd stood in the doorway, motionless, and of heading down the long dark hallway and noticing at the far end, the light behind the open living room door. Thinking of this left a strange impression. He went back to his reading.

That night, at about the same time, Roberto's partner at the publishing house, Jacobo Cruz, who was several years older than Roberto and, though he was a bit shorter than Roberto, was nonetheless a few pounds heavier, had just engaged, after a heap of trouble, in a bout of intercourse with a young black prostitute, whom he asked for her name. Sitting up and mechanically petting his head of short, just short of shaved-bald, hair, she told him her name, and then, even though he hadn't asked, volunteered her age— obviously and stupidly, Jacobo thought, subtracting a few years, as though a prostitute was never young enough. He stayed with her a little while longer, stroking her gleaming dark skin. Then he got dressed, stepped into the rainy night, and headed, as far as he could remember, in the direction of his parked car. He walked down one city street after another, under the slow-soaking, light autumn rain until he found at last the tree-lined avenue, which was completely deserted at that time of the night. He made his way up the avenue, stopping now and then to breathe in the clean, damp air, until he arrived at his car. He started the engine and set off down the long road, taking street after street until he came to his own and parked there. He went up to his apartment, and, when he opened the door, the silence and stillness inside was overwhelming. He went to the window and pushed it wide open. The night's silence was broken only by the chance sound of a far-off car. He knew he wouldn't be able to sleep that night. Slowly, the thoughts swirling in his head began to settle. First, he thought about the black girl, who was so tall and so thin and looked so frail. He thought of her body, which he'd been caressing a few minutes ago, and how different it was from the girl's eyes, as if it were far away from them. Vacant eyes, like the eyes of any hooker servicing a stranger who inspires nothing but disgust or fear, or, in the best of cases, indifference. Jacobo understood all that, and doing so had let loose a kind of inner unrest and self-loathing, which, in the end, he accepted, the way that little acts of egoism or small everyday perversions are accepted. Jacobo thought about the girl's skin, her black skin, and wondered how it was possible for him to have wanted her ever since he first saw her. A black girl, he repeated to himself, under his breath, barely parting his lips. Because Jacobo hated blacks. He hated homosexuals, too. And, like Céline, Jews.

He kept all this to himself, taking great care not to broach certain topics with Roberto, who, even though he knew about Jacobo's ill will toward certain minorities, considered it nothing more than a contrarian pose or show of bravado on the part of his friend, who deep down—he believed—didn't really think that way.

Jacobo remembered when he and Roberto met six years ago in a creative-writing workshop. Although at a glance they were two very different people, Jacobo had felt first sympathy and then a certain draw toward that tall and serious individual who was in the habit of dressing in a conventional, or to be honest, outmoded, style. He remembered Roberto's way of looking at people, that at first he had taken for haughtiness or contempt for others, but he came to understand was only a mask sheltering a vast bashfulness. He remembered their arguments about literature and life in which Roberto, who was the far more progressive thinker of the pair, seemed to shed all his reserve in wild flights of zeal, while Jacobo, in the end, always held back, keeping all his feelings and festering resentments pent up inside. And he remembered the year the idea to start a publishing house overtook them, that crazy venture they'd set out on, putting out a modest catalog they could feel proud of, although it now seemed likely to go up in smoke or deliberately bring them to ruin.

Several hours later, Abeba—which is also the name of her birth country's capital, and means "flower" in Ethiopian, and who is tall, very tall, like her city, and black like her city, like the night, like Africa—was feeling strange, too, like Roberto did after walking down the hall, and she gazed at the light behind the half-open door at the end of another dark hallway from the place where she lay in the darkness of her small bedroom. She curled up on a dirty mattress and stroked her stomach, and what she carried there, the seed of what one day would be her son, but at the time was the smallest hint of a bulge in her stomach. Then she fell asleep and dreamed of a man, at the far end of a dark hallway looking at her. And in her dream, Abeba knew this man would kill her; he would kill her and her son, the son she carried in her very guts, whom, were he to live, she would name Basbiel, after his father. She didn't dream any more that night.

Over the course of the next few days she had the same dream with a few variations. Sometimes the man would just stare at her from the other end of the hallway and the dream was soon over. Other times, she would tremble as she walked the long hallway toward him, and as she drew closer, his features began to change, mutating and transforming into other ones, and when she came up to him, the man would ask her if she was afraid, and she'd say yes, she was, but even though she knew she was about to die, she also knew that he understood her and she was somehow connected to him. Then she would kiss him, working his lips apart with her lips and tongue, feeling the dampness of his mouth, and then Abeba would wake up, open her eyes, and close them again, as she strained to find the bitter taste of the kiss from her dream still on her tongue, searching in herself, with no result, for the sense of peace she'd felt, which was bitter too, the peace held only by those who know they're going to die, and who understand that they must, and that to desire anything else is to desire in vain.

In the other variation of the dream, which she experienced only once, she walked toward not a man but a woman, who had white skin and dark hair and eyes, and the woman, who, even though she was very young, was leaning on a cane, asked her if she was afraid, as in the first version, and, as before, she answered yes, and then the woman told her not to be afraid, to think about things she liked, and Abeba said that she liked birds, birds and snakes, and the woman responded, saying that you can't like both birds and snakes, that she could understand why somebody might like birds, but not snakes. Abeba told the woman that she liked snakes because they could shed their skin, and the woman asked her if she wanted to shed her skin too, and Abeba said yes, and the woman told her that she was going to shed her skin too then, and as she said this she took out a knife from somewhere and first cut off Abeba's clothes, leaving her naked—in the dream Abeba was unable to move—and then cut off her black skin, pulling at it as she did, her hands at once firm and delicate, peeling away strips of bloody flesh, and even though Abeba felt a dreadful, deep, pointed, boundless pain, in her dream, while she bled to death, not a single scream left her lips. Because when you really want something, you can put up with anything, in dreams at least.

But Abeba's death wouldn't be like the one she'd dreamt that night in her miserable room in the whorehouse. Abeba would die a few months later, in the middle of the night, at the hands of somebody staring at her with eyes that were red and wet—not wet with tears of sadness, melancholy, or despair, but with other things, or in any case *not only with those things*—who would repeatedly slam her head against the bumper of a semitrailer at a highway rest stop, at the edge of a desert, and then savagely bisect her with a knife.

2.

Jacobo hadn't read Paula Boccia's manuscript when Roberto had, for days he hadn't even bothered to open his email. Around ten o' clock the following morning, Roberto called him and said that he should read it—right away. That was all he said. That and that they could meet the next day to talk about it. It was something Jacobo picked up in his friend's voice that made him pour a cup of coffee and head straight for his computer. He was all too familiar with Roberto, or at least he thought he was— with his way of saying things, and with the real meaning carried by a certain tone. He sat down at his computer and drank the cup of coffee, then went to the liquor cabinet for something else. At three o'clock he went down to get some food. As he stepped out of the elevator, he suddenly found himself face-to-face with a woman who'd been waiting to go up. They were in an unlit place, and when the woman saw him, she jumped. Jacobo met her eyes staring back at him. Her pupils were dilated. As he was leaving the build- ing, he tried to forget that image, those pale eyes—blue or maybe gray—to think of other eyes, to picture the look of another's eyes: Paula Boccia's eyes. Of course, he thought, hers would have to be dark. And there was no doubt in his mind that if he'd ambushed her in the half-lit lobby, she wouldn't have given him that startled look—it would've been one of curiosity or boredom or almost anything, but not fear.

When he got back home, he called Roberto's cell phone, and they made plans to meet at Jacobo's place at nine. After he'd hung up, it occurred to him how stupid it had been to invite Roberto over rather than meet up, as usual, at his friend's pristine apartment. Now he'd have to clean things up, at least a little, or at the very least air it out, and he'd need some decent wine on hand so he could offer his friend a glass, or at bare minimum some good vermouth, and not the rotgut whiskey he was used to drinking. He mulled over how much he'd been spending lately, over the course of the last few weeks, during those nightly excursions that were getting longer and longer, always ending in something different, something different but still the same, only a little more . . . a little more . . . but Jacobo understood that there wasn't any fitting adjective and that this was all it was: a little more. And it seemed then as if his whiskey wasn't so bad, no, it wasn't so bad after all, in fact, he said to himself, his whiskey was excellent. As he said this to himself, he looked out the window at the light growing red and dim, and then he looked at the bottle on the dining room table and at the half-open dining room door, which led to the hallway, and through the open door at the other end he could just barely make out the kitchen, and could see, just slightly from that angle, the kitchen sink full of dirty glasses and a few plates, also dirty. And he looked down at his hands and thought: I'm poorer than a church mouse.

Of course, that wasn't strictly true, only subjectively true. According to the self-pitying and, perhaps to some extent, self-pacifying way Jacobo saw himself, it was true.

"I'm poorer than a church mouse," Paula Boccia was also sighing to herself, as she sat on a bench in Madrid-Barajas Airport, mentally reviewing the money at her disposal and the expenses she'd be up against in the next few weeks. She had her uncle's address. Her mother had primly written it down for her in green ink on a scrap of paper. She made a rough estimate of the number of days she could get by without the financial assistance of her uncle Manuel—her mother's only living sibling—who for years had been living in Madrid. He was a widower several years older than her mother, and muddled along on a humble pension. It was funny, Paula reflected, to think that her uncle could help her out and keep her on her feet while she was trying to make a life for herself here in Madrid, when—she assumed—he barely had enough for himself.

Paula walked slowly, having no alternative, leaning on her walking stick, toward a vending machine. She chose a drink, put in some change, and pressed the corresponding button. The can fell with a clang. She leaned on the machine to bend down a little and, performing this maneuver with apparent discomfort and strain, retrieved the can. She had settled on a lemon-lime soda. The can was light yellow, and the letters of the brand name and flavor were in white. A delicate green line twisted all around it, depicting stalks and leaves. The design reminded her of the delicate touch with which her mother had written down her uncle's address.

"Why are you writing in green? For God's sake, Mom!" she'd said.

"What difference does it make, Paula? I like green, I've always liked green. I like colors."

"But who writes in green? It's so tacky. People write in blue or black. It's . . . it's hideous."

"The closer you get to death, the more you want colors around, it's like—"

"What's that got to do with it!" Paula cut in, scowling, but she immediately retreated when she saw the expression

on the face of her mother, who was looking at her the way
you'd look at something that didn't meet your expecta-
tions, something familiar that's changed. She looked at her
the way one looks at somebody one loves, and hasn't seen
in a long time, who's now somebody else, another person, and a worse one. The way you'd look at a lover from
years ago whom you haven't seen in a long time, while at
the wake of this person, whom you've come to pay your
respects to, because you've found out by chance that she's
died and where the funeral is being held. So you go, and
nobody there knows you, or maybe they do, only they're
pretending not to, and you look at her husband, at his
ravaged face, and it's clear that he really doesn't know you,
but you recognize him: he's the same person she'd pointed
out to you in her pictures, the person she'd told you about
countless times while the two of you smoked, having just
made love, only he's older and fatter and a little more bald,
and he stares back at you, wondering who you are, as if
waiting for you to say something, something you don't say,
and you slowly walk over to the open coffin at an angle
where all you can see is her white profile, her straight nose,
her white dress, and you move closer until you can see her,
you look at her face, and you can't take your eyes off her,
off her closed eyes, her mouth, it's impossible. And that's
how it feels. That's just how it feels.

Paula erased this image from her mind. Erased her
mother's staring face. She concentrated, instead, on the
cloying, acid tang of the soda. She'd always missed those
lemon-lime soft drinks from her childhood that left a bitter taste in her mouth. This one left only a sweet, artificial
flavor. Sipping at the can, she headed back to the bench
where she'd been sitting. She dropped her backpack by her

feet and heaved herself once again onto the bench, cursing under her breath the complete lack of armrests. She tried to relax, to shut out the persistent, albeit faint, ache that she was feeling and had been feeling ever since she left Buenos Aires. She tried to clear her mind. She had to decide where to go, what to do. She figured she'd have a little time, a few weeks, as many days as the money stashed in a hidden pocket in her backpack would allow. Maybe she could even put off meeting her uncle for a while, she thought. Stretch out that time a few extra days or weeks or maybe forever. She could live alone, take care of herself. She could find a job, however miserable, or maybe even sell her body—she felt capable of it. She knew she wasn't ugly, quite the opposite. You wouldn't call her tall, but she was a more or less considerable height, slim, and had neat black hair and big dark eyes. She felt capable of arousing men. But then she thought to herself: No, that sort of thing's impossible. After all, who wants to sleep with a one-legged whore?

Paula hadn't answered a single one of the emails Roberto Fate had sent her. It had been days since she'd last checked her account. She hadn't answered any of his phone calls, either. Paula assumed it was her uncle calling, or else some acquaintance of her mother. In fact, during the first days she spent in Madrid, Paula didn't answer any calls at all. She was staying at the cheapest boardinghouse she could find, which was run by an old Galician woman, who, despite all the years she'd been living in the capital, had still retained her accent. Paula had a small room with a tiny window that looked out on a minuscule courtyard. She had access to a filthy kitchen and a bathroom, both of which she shared with an elderly couple who said they were tourists: a Romanian man around fifty whom she'd never heard say one word and a young skinny guy who was silent, too, but less so than the Romanian. Sometimes, but only sometimes—his room shared a wall with hers—she could hear him crying in the night.

Of course, Paula wasn't expecting anyone to call her about publishing the manuscript she'd sent to a handful of Spanish publishing houses. She'd received several frustrating responses, and hadn't heard back at all from other presses, and although she'd closely studied which publishers to send her work to, she was no longer harboring any hopes. In spite of her twenty-six years, this was her fourth book, her second of fiction. Early on, she had written two books of poetry, both—more so the second—of an initiatory and narrative cast. After her second book, which like the first, she was unable to publish—except for a few poems in a more or less local anthology of young Buenos Aires poets—her mother threw her father out of the house. She remembered it clearly. She remembered her mother yelling at him, saying that she couldn't take it anymore, that life was something else, not whatever this was, that she was done putting up with his instability, his always being on the edge of a cliff, his *I'm not feeling well*—all of it. She remembered how she had made him breakfast, and how her mother had told him that when he was done with it he could be on his way, she would go pack his things, and she remembered how at first her father wouldn't even take a bite of his breakfast, but eventually he started and ate the whole thing, as if he was forcing it down, and Paula knew that he was only eating it because she'd made it, and that every bite her father choked down felt as if it was burning his throat, nauseating him, but he choked it down to the last crumb and then kissed Paula and turned as if to go to the bedroom, where his wife was, but heard her talking to herself and moaning, and in the end he just stood there not knowing what to do and turned back around and kissed his daughter again. He told her that he would come by later for his things and he would talk with Mom and say goodbye to her, since he knew there was nothing that could be done anymore, nothing that could be fixed, and he left. And he didn't come by later. He didn't come by ever again.

Her first book of fiction, *Skins*, was a novel made of distinct parts in which various desperate characters, although at first they didn't seem to realize it, would try to escape from their own bodies, their own skins, searching for comfort in any other skin. In her novel, the different stories developed in parallel toward a common end, in which sex seemed to be only a pretext for the main characters to go further in a strange quest where cruelty, sexual domination, and a trace of something that could be considered a kind of cannibalism—it was left rather unclear whether this really happened or was only a metaphor—created a thick, dark atmosphere. The book was put out by an independent publisher in Buenos Aires, but few noticed, and the sales were sparse.

She began writing her fourth and most recent book, her second work of fiction, at the same time her mother fell ill, and completed the book as the illness progressed. Although at first Paula had set her mind on writing her second novel, whose whole structure she'd outlined when she began writing it, the emotional strain of her mother's illness—in which stable periods, sometimes lasting no more than a day, alternated with unbearably painful bouts of depression—drained her of whatever strength and self-control she might have had left to maintain the thread of style required by a novel. And so, what in the beginning was going to be a novel turned into a jumbled series of short stories that jettisoned any clean or clear narrative structure, tending instead to the chaotic, and, in a certain way—she later thought—to the human, to pain, and at the same time, to pleasure, to the beauty and the stench that always followed close behind.

A month before her mother died, she'd sent the manuscript to a number of Spanish publishers, and since then she'd been receiving impersonal letters of rejection, and the odd one or two that passed along the dim hope that perhaps the manuscript had been read. During the last months of her mother's life, she had decided to leave Buenos Aires, to leave Argentina. Then her mother died and after the burial, Paula stayed in the house for a few days, praying to a God she didn't believe in, but in whom her mother had devoutly, and they weren't so much prayers as conversations with the idea of God that seemed to linger in the air of her house, around her mother's bed, under the crucifix that hung on the wall, in the rooms where the venetian blinds were always slanted half-shut, in the shadows. After that, Paula decided she would never write anything ever again.

3.

Jacobo was with Roberto until quite late that night. Since there was hardly anything to eat at Jacobo's, they had decided—that is, Roberto had decided—they should go out for some dinner.

"Don't worry," Roberto said, "it's on me." Jacobo glanced at his friend, expecting to be met with a look of irony, but was comforted to find no hint of any such thing. So they left and went to a quiet restaurant they knew, although given that it was a Wednesday night, all the restaurants in Almería were quiet. They talked at length about the manuscript, which, more than anything else, had surprised them. Roberto listed all the things he liked about it, things that, at the same time, he found quite disturbing, and he mentioned the author's way of playing games with the reader, toying with him, making him judge, jump to conclusions, only to confront him directly later on, as if she were staring him in the face. Then he talked about the possible adjustments he would make to the text, maybe getting rid of some Argentine expressions. Jacobo, on the other hand, said he wouldn't lay a finger on so much as a comma. Later, over a few drinks at a pub near Roberto's place, Roberto told Jacobo about his unsuccessful attempts to contact the author, and they delved into a discussion about how to get in touch with her and what course of action was best.

At one in the morning they said goodbye. Roberto headed back to his apartment and Jacobo was left to his own devices. He walked along the cold streets without any intention of heading home. Like a zombie, he wandered the wet sidewalks, on the lookout for open bars. He walked down Calle Rambla Obispo Orberá and turned left when he came to Calle San Leonardo, where he remembered there was a bar that often played good music. Finally, at the end of the street, after he'd abandoned hope of finding it, he saw the bar, which now went by a different name. He went inside, and even though the place was more or less the same as before, something had changed, something that Jacobo couldn't help but think was significant. Still, the man serving drinks at the bar was the same. Jacobo greeted him and, almost from a sense of duty—he'd regretted going in the moment he crossed the threshold—he ordered a drink. He sat down for a while, listening to the music and looking at the customers, what few there were, talking among themselves—far away from it all, from the damp, Jacobo thought. He noticed a woman, fiftysomething, smoking by herself and looking back at him. Then he left.

He followed the street that intersected his own and turned down several side streets, until he got to where he wanted to go. He'd come to a nightclub. It was called Essence. He pushed open the black-and-red door and went inside. The room was dark and several spotlights swept their beams across the floor. Club music was playing and it was turned up loud. Jacobo greeted the blond girl behind the bar, who was talking, or trying to talk, with a couple of men holding drinks and smoking. She looked at him, ignored his greeting, and went on talking with the other two men, whose eyes never left the girl's cleavage. At the opposite end of the bar there was another man leaning forward on his forearms, drinking. Jacobo said hello and sat down beside him. He was the owner of the place, and Jacobo knew him by sight from his past nights there. He ordered a whiskey, and while the girl served him he looked at the two guys who hadn't stopped chatting and laughing with the bargirl. One of them looked back with a sneer full of contempt and disdain. He ignored them and exchanged a few words with the man sitting beside him.

After his fifth whiskey, Jacobo looked at the younger guy, who was no longer talking with anyone—the bargirl was making something and his friend had left—he smiled and said: "That makes five, it's a record." The other man looked down at his drink.

Then Jacobo became dizzy and things took on a glint of unreality.

A middle-aged woman walked in and made a beeline for the owner of the bar. She started talking to him very nervously, holding her arm out toward the bargirl and pointing at her. The bargirl, for her part, shouted something at the owner, which he answered with a snort, standing so quickly that he knocked over his barstool. At that point, Jacobo's head began to swim, and he got up from his stool too without any clear idea what he'd do next, knowing only that something was about to happen. Then he felt his stomach give a tremendous heave and he headed as fast as he could for the bathroom, closed the door, and vomited in the toilet. Faced with the whitish liquid and his own bile, he gave another retch, but this time nothing came up. Then he heard the banging on the door, reverberating as if the person were trying to knock it off the hinges, or as if somebody desperate were trying to escape from something horrible, to escape from the purest terror, and just wanted him to open the door. And Jacobo understood that the horror was out there, with the person who was knocking. Horror was on the other side of the door.

From here on, this story changes. It becomes something else.

From here on, this story—which, even though it's not a story about violence, does contain violence—changes, it takes another path. Or as Bolaño wrote in his "Days of 1978," *This is where the story should end, but life is a little harder than literature.* Or perhaps a little crueler than literature, more violent.

Sometimes things begin or change with someone's knocking on the other side of a door, and so, as Jacobo stood listening to the banging on the door of the bathroom he was holed up in, everything changed and took another, drastically different course. It all veered straight into violence and horror. And even though it would be too great a coincidence, one can imagine that at that same time, at that same exact moment, although it probably didn't happen like this, that Paula Boccia, also holed up in a bathroom, heard somebody banging desperately on the other side of the door. Somebody who was, no doubt, terrified as well, and running away from something, from something horrible that also could have been there, at that moment, on the other side of the door.

But let's return to the Essence nightclub, let's return to the moment Jacobo heard somebody, who seemed terrified or trying to escape from terror, banging with all their might on the bathroom door, as if inside that vile bathroom lay their salvation. And Jacobo opened the door and found himself facing the bargirl, her eyes open wide, so wide it seemed impossible, her face struck him as somehow abnormal, changed, almost shapeless, and then Jacobo realized that the girl's jaw had been broken. Then he noticed the blood on her hands that grabbed for Jacobo's shirt, staining it, and then he saw the barstool and the man, the club owner with bloodshot eyes, his face flecked in his own spit, lifting the stool and bringing it down with all his might on the back of the girl, who was still latched onto Jacobo, her eyes open so wide it seemed as if her eyelids were missing, and he saw her snap forward, as if she'd been split in two, and then he heard her scream and collapse and claw at the floor trying to get up but slipping on her own blood, and then he saw the man again, standing next to her, panting and taking in breath as if he were about to burst, and he saw him stomping the girl's legs, her torso, her head, and then the girl managed to scramble to her feet, but the man caught hold of her and made her look at him and spat in her face. And then he let her go, and she fell to the floor and crawled away gasping, blood masking her face and streaming from her mouth, until she reached the door and escaped. Jacobo stood perfectly still, looking at the other man, who was breathing noisily, his open shirt revealing thick black hair covering a white chest, that inhaled and exhaled, rising and falling like a motor piston.

When Paula Boccia heard somebody knocking desperately on the bathroom door, she was washing herself in the tub. She had just used the facilities: urinated and defecated, something she tried to put off as long as possible, to avoid having to visit the bathroom too often. In order to urinate, she needed to remove her prosthetic leg from her stump, and the process of undoing the straps and buckles, urinating, and snapping everything back into place never took less than twenty-five minutes. Because of this, she would contain herself for as long as possible and always try to teach her body the habit of performing necessities when it was time to bathe. Because of this Paula Boccia didn't answer—didn't even make a sound, holding her breath—when somebody tried to open the locked bathroom door, and then started banging on it, loudly and repeatedly;

because it would have been complicated for her to get out of the bathtub and reattach her prosthetic leg, but maybe also because of surprise or fear.

When Paula ventured to open the door, after putting her orthopedic leg back in place, she was confronted by a silent, dark, empty hallway. She walked toward her room, but as she was about to open her door, another door opened, the one at the end of the hallway, the one to the room of the tall, thin Romanian man who never spoke. And there he appeared, doubled over, with his shirt unbuttoned and his hands clutching a stomach that seemed not to exist, not to be there at all, beneath hairy flesh that sunk in between the ribs that were about to rip, cut through it, and be free of this dead skin like a snake. Paula stood frozen on the spot as she watched the man dart out hunched over, leaning against the hallway wall, toward the bathroom, and then clutching the bathroom doorknob. She saw a spasm run the length of the Romanian's body before he dropped to his knees, coming down with a heavy thud that could have fractured his kneecaps, and maybe did, but it's not as if that mattered anymore, and then the man opened his mouth and vomited an enormous amount of blood and bile onto the floor. After a few surprised, terrified moments, Paula's first reaction was to think of getting her phone and calling an ambulance, but she decided to attend to the man first, in case there was something she could do right there, herself. She went over and grabbed him under the armpits, hanging her cane from her wrist by the strap on the handle, putting it to the side, and using the wall for support. The Romanian, noticing the pressure of her hands, lifted his head and looked at her, but his eyes didn't see, or if they did, it was something else they saw, a memory of the past or of the future, because when a person is about to die sooner than he'd thought, he can remember things from the life he's about to be cheated out of living.

Even though the Romanian's body was almost weight-less, as she tugged it along, Paula felt a shooting pain where the stump fit into the prosthesis. Panting from her exer-tions, she managed to drag him back to his room and throw him onto the bed, then, as she paused for a second to recover her strength and think of what to do next, she looked at the man lying there on the dirty sheets. She could see that he hadn't eaten in days, weeks, and she could see that he was dying and that it was too late to do anything about it now that there was no longer anything anyone could do for him. Despite this thought, Paula gathered the strength to stand up and go to the hallway to get some help and her cell phone. Then she heard something. The faint sound of crying from behind the door of the room beside her own softly broke the night's silence. She went to the door and listened closer to the crying, hearing it more clearly now. Then she knocked and without waiting for an answer turned the doorknob and opened the door to the room of the young man who would cry at night.

When she entered the room, she smelled a strong, omnipresent funk. She felt the thick air and the stench come in through her nostrils, and suppressed a retch. The boy's room was covered in clothes scattered across the floor, along with paper scraps, towels, newspapers, all of it dirty, blackened, stained, and then Paula realized, in hor-ror, that everything was covered in shit. There were feces smeared over the floor, across the wall, into the towels and sheets tossed on the ground. Then, in a corner, she saw the boy, naked, his whole body covered in bruises and sores, squatting, raw flesh on his back, shivering, sobbing, and rocking himself back and forth with an autistic stare. From his mouth streamed a fine, never-ending thread of saliva that merged with the smeared shit at his feet.

Paula closed the door to the boy's room and went as fast as she could, her orthopedic leg dragging along, to her room, found her phone, and dialed the emergency number. She spoke slowly, choking back tears, struggling to vocalize. Then she went back to the Romanian's room. She went to the bed and looked at him. His chest seemed to have stopped moving, and his jutting ribs were motionless under the hirsute skin, skin that looked as if a snake had sprouted hair. Paula brought her hand to the skin, brushing first past the long black hairs on the man's chest, until her fingers came into contact with his white skin, withered but gleaming with the glow of a sick man's skin, or rather, that of a man who's sick and about to die, or maybe a man who's already dead, and this glow . . . simply the last light of a body that's already been abandoned by almost everything. And indeed, the skin was as cold as a snake's. She drew her hand back and slumped down in a chair, exhausted, feeling as if she'd gone several nights without sleep, her nerves shot. She let herself cry a little, sobbing until she finally calmed down. Then, while she waited for the ambulance, even though her tongue felt swollen and her mouth was parched, she spoke on the phone with the owner of the boardinghouse. After that, completely defeated, she gave in and dialed the number that had repeatedly called her over the last few days, that she hadn't answered, the number she believed to be her uncle's. And on the other end of the line, Roberto Fate answered.

4.

"The life of a policeman is, sometimes, hard. Sometimes a policeman has to root around in the filth, live with it, be so close and so connected to it that it starts leaching into him, into his skin, under his fingernails. Being a policeman is like working in a fish market. The smell of fish clings to your skin, your hair, above all your hair. That's why I shaved my head, because of the stench. That's why when I get home I scrub myself under a stream of hot water, almost scalding myself, until my skin is rosy red. That way it's almost erased, it almost disappears, not completely, but almost. The problem's inside. I know none of this matters to you, it doesn't matter to you one damn little bit. But, you know, you aren't in any position, are you? you aren't in any position to tell me to shut up. Nope, not you. You're the hooker, I'm the policeman. You're the junkie, I'm the policeman. You're what's barely left of a life annihilated by disaster and you can talk about it with anybody who might want to listen to a tired old whore, but I'm the police-man. So now you're going to listen to me. I wanted to be a policeman, true, and I was mistaken, but by the time I knew that, it was too late to do anything about it, to turn back, to get away, to run off, so I tried to arrange things so there'd be some distance between me and the filth, terror, and madness. That's why I pushed myself, really pushed myself, and in the end I pulled it off and got promoted to inspector. It wasn't easy trying to get myself out of the shit. It was hard as hell getting over to the sidelines, but I made it there with my brains, and with perseverance and putting in the time and working through exhaustion and knowing how to deal with people, that's how I made it and got to be an inspector. I managed to get off the beats, off the night patrols, the late-night calls, the ugly, busted-up, terrified faces, the vomit, the blood, the sight of unbearable pain, the urge, finally, of wanting to deliver the coup de grâce and not being able to, and calling a doctor. A doctor! Seeing death and life and what's left when life goes, evaporates and isn't there anymore, and the worst thing of all is that you don't have to be dead for that to happen," the policeman said.

She moved in the bed, pulling off the sheets covering her body, and, wearing only a thong, crawled across the mattress toward the chair he was sitting in.

"Don't try it, I'm a fag," the policeman said.

"Don't even try it, I'm a fucking fag," the policeman said.

"I'm a goddamn fucking fag," the policeman said.

And she stayed still, very still, for a second or two, watching the policeman, and then smoothed her hair and went back to where she'd been, pulling the sheets over herself. He continued:

"That's right, they called me a fucking fag, and I bit my tongue. Candy-ass fag they called me, and I still bit my tongue. I didn't say anything, I was an inspector, I investigated, gave orders, I bit my tongue because I didn't want to go back on the beat, I didn't want to go back to the filth. So I ran my hand over my shaved head, over my white head, and looked down and shut up. He was the one who said it to me, in front of everybody: Abdul, Martínez, Pino, Inspector González, who was still bleeding a little with a broken nose . . . everybody. He, Victor, he looked me in the eye and he called me a fucking fag. He looked at me with those big dark eyes of his, and, moving his pink, fleshy lips, he talked at me, and I couldn't stop staring at those lips I'd wanted so much. I wouldn't have said anything to him, not a word, but what had happened that night got the better of me, it'd shattered my nerves, thrown me off balance, and the very second we parked the squad car in the station garage I wound up confessing to him, and in that exact instant I knew I'd made a fatal mistake."

The last rays of evening light were finally giving way to a dull, beaten dark beyond the window. The policeman kept talking:

"The black guy was named Basbiel, but I found that out later, afterward, when some other black guy creeped up on me in the doorway of that grimy house and asked me if the dude was dead. I told him he was and asked if he knew the guy, and he nodded and said his name was Basbiel, and I took him by the arm and squeezed hard, because I was worked up and because I felt powerless and above all because I was hopeless, and he told me that he didn't know anything, that he barely even knew Basbiel, except that he was a good guy who'd had a dream about his wife and son and he'd been trying to find them ever since he came to Spain, but he'd never met his son because he'd separated from them before the kid was born, and that because of this dream he'd gone crazy. So I asked if he knew what Basbiel saw in his dream, and he said Basbiel saw his wife and son being killed, and I wanted to ask him more, but he slipped away into the shadows, into the night, into poverty, which is black, too. And now I remember how it all started. I was going with Victor in the car to pick up some reports, that was it, but then a call came in over the radio and we were right there, not a mile from the ghetto, and he said: We're here, we've got to go. And

I said: It's not our job. And he said: We have to go. And
I said: We've got things to do, other things. And he said:
But we're policemen, good policemen. That settled it, so
he turned the steering wheel and took us off the highway
and toward the projects. In the wide stretch of gravel, in
front of the miserable houses, there was already a squad
car parked, and just when we stopped, Pino and Martínez
pulled up behind us. They said hello to me, called me
inspector, and stared at me for a second, waiting for me
to say something, give some order, but I didn't say a word.
So they walked up to the door and took out their guns.
Victor followed them and so did I, and I unholstered my
gun, too. The door was open and we heard the voices of
Abdul and Inspector González ordering somebody to get
on the ground and stay still and we went inside, and there
he was, Basbiel, tall, sinewy, thin, and reeking of sweat and
shit and madness. He looked like he was out of his gourd,
his eyes were completely bloodshot and wide open, and he
opened them even wider, which I thought was impossible,
and then he said something, something we didn't understand, while González kept telling him over and over to
get on the ground and stay still. Then González looked
at us and saw us pointing our guns at the black guy and
said: Easy, boys, easy, no need to get excited, and took a
step toward the black guy and started saying something
in a calm tone, something we didn't catch, and then the
black guy made a quick move and his long, unusually
long arm shot out and he caught González by the hair
with one hand and smashed him in the face with the
other, and González, whose nose was broken and spurting
blood, collapsed at the black guy's feet, and the guy started
screaming in a booming voice that seemed to come from

nowhere and everywhere all at once: Abeba, Abeba, Abeba! he screamed and we were all scared shitless, wondering what the black guy was saying, and then Abdul, fucking dumbass Abdul, our Arabic interpreter, said: He's going to kill him, he's screaming that he's going to kill him, and we all opened fire, on a hair trigger, because we're good policemen. Martínez aimed for the arm, of course, because Martínez always aims for arms or legs, but he missed, and Abdul and Victor shot for the stomach or head, because they always shot to kill, but they missed, although one of their bullets brushed the black guy's shoulder, and I shot to miss, off to the black guy's right, but my aim was bad, and my bullet hit Basbiel, killing him with a shot to the head. He fell backward, and at first I just stood there, and then I thought about what the black guy had been screaming, because I'm a good policeman and I've trained my mind to pay attention to details, and I remembered that Abeba was the capital of Ethiopia, and then I snapped out of it because I understood everything, and I turned to Abdul and yelled: Fucking sand-sucking son of a bitch, he was talking in Ethiopian, not Arabic, why the fuck did you say he was going to kill González! And then everything went blurry and I remember that Martínez grabbed me before I jumped on Abdul, and then it's all a blank, and all I remember is that later, in the squad car, with Victor driving while the others waited for the ambulance, I was torn up, totally torn up inside, and Victor parked the car in the garage and grabbed my shoulder and reached his other hand out to touch my face, and then I told him."

5.

Roberto Fate hung up the telephone after talking with Paula, sat on the couch, and stayed there for a long time, staring at the white wall, which was in need of a coat of paint. He stared without seeing, or seeing something other than what was before him, at the small cracks and the water stains on the wall that faced north. Then somebody knocked at the door. Roberto opened it and found himself facing Jacobo. A Jacobo who didn't seem himself, as if in a daze, looking like a robot. The only answer he gave to Roberto's "What's going on?" was a vacant stare, before he pushed past him into the living room, where he took a seat on the old couch.

Roberto could see that something serious had happened to his friend, and because he knew him well, he also saw that he wasn't about to talk about it, and that he shouldn't ask, either. So he turned on the TV, which he hardly ever watched, and the flat images followed each other in front of Jacobo's flat stare. For an hour, they watched newscasters repeat the same thing over and over. Then a stupid game show came on, featuring questions that Jacobo almost always answered before the contestant did, until with a "That's enough!" Roberto turned off the TV.

"I spoke on the phone with Paula, she's in Madrid and she's coming here in a few days to talk with us about her manuscript," he blurted.

Jacobo stared at him, motionless, as if he hadn't quite managed to comprehend what Roberto had said, or as if he simply couldn't believe it.

"I'm hungry," he finally announced.

In the kitchen, they browsed the canned food. Roberto

never cooked, and if he wasn't going out to eat at some cheap restaurant, he'd either eat fresh fruit, which he always had lying around, or canned food. They ate in silence. Over coffee, Jacobo asked if Roberto had anything new to read. They went to the living room, and Roberto took a book down from the shelves.

"Here, it's *The Witness* by Juan Villoro," he said.

"What have you been reading?" Jacobo asked.

"I wanted to start *The Angel of Darkness*."

"Well, shit," he said and went to the bedroom with Villoro's *The Witness*, and Roberto, who didn't know what to think about what his friend meant by this "Well, shit," in turn took from its shelf the book by Sábato and made himself comfortable on the sofa. And the whole evening went by like this, Jacobo reading and Roberto, who was finding it hard to focus on his book, simply feeling happy, an abstract happiness whose source he didn't know or understand. During these moments, he thought about this happiness, about whether he owed it to having found Paula Boccia, the author of that wonderful, strange book they hoped to publish, or whether this happiness had nothing to do with her and came instead from the fact that everything was now falling into place in the puzzle of his life. And he thought that now it felt more rational that he'd gone through with the crazy idea of founding a literary publishing house, but he didn't know whether that was just because he'd strengthened his friendship with Jacobo by being able to embark on a life project with him, or simply because his friend was there now, lying in his bedroom, reading Villoro's *The Witness*.

When Roberto, who was still absorbed in his thoughts, let his eyes wander back to the page in front of him, he could no longer make out the words, so he got up from the sofa, and turned on the floor lamp. Under the weak yellow light, he was still unable to concentrate on the book and spent some time thinking about Paula Boccia, that strange woman. Then he remembered a fragment from *The Third Reich*, one of the first Bolaño novels to give a glimpse of what would come later, in his mature writing. In that novel, the protagonist, a young German oddball who loved war games and Goethe's poetry, takes a vacation on the Costa Brava with his girlfriend. This vacation seems to extend indefinitely and, although his girlfriend returned to Germany, the protagonist refuses to go back and report to his job and his life. Udo—that was the young German's name—felt hopelessly attracted to the mysterious owner of the hotel where he was staying, an older married woman, also German, whose husband was dying of cancer, and with whom he had a strange romantic understanding. When she chided Udo for staying and said he should return to his own life, go back to Germany for his own good, to take care of himself and not her, he told her: You are Germany. Roberto remembered how affected he'd been by the young German's answer. Although, later, meditating on the book, he recognized that although there were much more intense narrative moments, that phrase, that answer of young Udo's, filled him with a huge emotion. And he somehow associated that phrase with Paula Boccia, though he understood how incongruous this was, and that Paula didn't have—couldn't have—the remotest thing to do with Germany. Then he thought about what Paula would look like, what kind of face she'd have, the color of her eyes, what her hair would be like, her features . . . her features, needless to say, wouldn't be German. He fantasized about her body, her hands. He imagined white skin and pale-colored eyes, maybe green, and delicate hands with long fingers, and Slavic features, definitely, he thought, but of course that was impossible, since even if he couldn't remember in his daydreaming if Paula was Argentine or Chilean or Mexican or Uruguayan, in any case she was South American and what she certainly wasn't was Russian or Ukrainian, and therefore she couldn't have Slavic features. But then he thought, Why not? Why couldn't she be a Russian-Uruguayan or a Russian-Argentine or Russian-Mexican or Russian-Chilean? And in his half-conscious state, Roberto said to Paula:

"You are Russia."

When he came back to himself, or rather, to the consciousness of himself—which are two different things—Roberto closed the book that was open on his knees and went to the bedroom, where he found his friend sound asleep on top of the covers, fully dressed.

Roberto untucked the sheets, being careful not to wake him. He stripped down to his underwear and then started undressing Jacobo.

"Hey, what are you doing?" Jacobo said sleepily, opening his eyes.

"I was taking off your clothes so you could sleep. I'm going to the couch."

"Can you stay, please?" Jacobo asked.

"Okay, but don't try anything or else," he said jokingly to his friend.

"Don't worry, I'm barely able to with a woman," he said, in a tone that, while ironic, didn't match the seriousness of his face.

Already on one occasion, Jacobo had confessed to Roberto the problems he'd been having in recent months with his sex life, an issue around which a kind of vow of silence had formed after a bitter monologue Jacobo had unleashed in response to his friend's offer to help. But Roberto knew that that wasn't it, it was something else, something Jacobo had done, or rather, Roberto suspected, something he'd found, something so pivotal, at least in Jacobo's eyes, that it was impossible to stumble on it by chance, something that's found only after a painstaking search. But he didn't mention a word of this to Jacobo. Instead, he simply got into bed next to his friend's flabby body, pulled the sheets over himself, and turned out the light. And just as the weight of sleep pressed Roberto's eyelids shut in the dark bedroom, he heard Jacobo's voice beside him:

"It's odd about Paula's last name. Boccia is a game, a game for cripples."

And with this last sentence echoing in his head, Roberto closed his eyes, and a deep, heavy sleep drowned his mind.

Roberto didn't dream about Paula Boccia that night. For the first time since he'd read her manuscript, he dreamt about another woman, a black woman, and the dream disturbed him and left him in a state of surprise, that, if not identical, was at least quite similar to the state Paula and Jacobo were in after their brutal encounters with violence and terror.

In his dream, Roberto, in the half-dark with a light at his back, was watching as a tall, thin black girl was advancing through what he at first thought was a cave or tunnel with a light at the end. Then he realized that it was a long, dark hallway, and the light was coming from two rooms at the beginning and the end of it. The woman walked shakily toward where Roberto was standing and reached out to him with a hand whose long, black, delicate fingers were also shaking, and Roberto heard words coming out of his mouth, although he didn't remember saying them, it was as if another mind was using his lips and all he could do was listen. The voice said: Don't be nervous, whatever has to happen will happen. He took a deep breath, and this time it really was him breathing, filling his lungs with air. Then the voice said: Take my hand, and his hand obeyed the voice's words, and the girl, who obeyed them too, took his hand, and the voice said: Let's go, and he started walking, and she went with him, to the illuminated room, where there was an open window. Standing in the room and looking out the window, he saw tall buildings on one side and on the other side an iron structure that looked like a bridge. She went up to the window too, and then he smelled something that was a combination of the smell of his sweat mixed with the smell of her sweat mixed with something else, something else that he couldn't place; it smelled like stagnant, filthy, dead water. She closed the window and turned around. Her body was right next to his, her mouth nearly touching his. He could feel her breath and he breathed it in, and he had the strange feeling that she was his, and then she asked him a question, a question that Roberto already knew. And that's when he did it.

When he woke, Roberto had forgotten the question the young black woman asked him in his dream, but what he didn't forget was her face and her long, thin body, strong but fragile, and what he couldn't forget, either, was what, in the dream, he'd done. It was etched in his mind. He reconstructed the situation over and over again in his head, obsessing over her black skin, the cadence of her movements, the sour smell of sweat, and another smell that mixed with his own and with the smell of fear and the smell of insanity: The smell of misery? The smell of mankind? The stench of mankind? The perfume of mankind? It smelled like sex, and then like guts, it was like indifference, like unhappiness, and at the same time like happiness, like succumbing flesh, and like pleasure, and pain.

The dream had left Roberto feeling unsettled. Something inside him told him the woman was real, that she existed somewhere, somewhere nearby. He thought about himself and what he'd done in the dream, what he'd done with his own hands. He thought about the place where it all happened, about that hallway, about that high-ceilinged room. And he thought about what he'd seen from the window, about that metal structure that looked like an enormous, rusted old bridge.

6.

As daylight dimmed, it left a cold fluorescence, and in this light Roberto thought about the times when we feel that life is putting us to the test, and he knew that all those times he'd felt this were false, and that this was the real moment that life had chosen to test him.

He tried to remember the exact angle from which he'd seen the metal structure's rusted girders in his dream. Then he slowly examined the different parts of the metal bridge or pier, it turned out, that jutted into the port, with railroad tracks running alongside it to a loading bay. It had been in disuse since 1973, but in its time, this pier, that was known as El Cable Inglés, was used to load cargo ships with iron ore from the Alquife Mines. At the stoplight, he crossed the wide avenue that separated El Cable Inglés from the buildings on the other curb, all of considerable height. He took his time, walking down the sidewalk and stopping to look at the rusted loading bay from different points along the way, trying to picture the angle he'd seen the pier from in his dream, and imagining the views one would have of it from different heights. It took a long time. The first building he thought he'd been looking from in his dream had to be discarded after realizing it was a more recent construction than what he remembered dreaming. He got rid of two of the five buildings this way and was left with the three oldest. In the end, by moving around from one point to another, he was sure that the room he'd dreamt of was in a building of reddish brick about nine stories high. He walked back and forth in front of the facade until he settled on the horizontal angle he'd been looking from. Then he mulled over the vertical angle until he determined that he must have been on the third or fourth floor.

He waited outside the building's main entrance, and before long somebody came out. He rushed to catch the door and held it open as an old woman emerged; he smiled at her as she left. He slipped inside the front door, which was surprisingly clean, and decided to take the stairs up to the fourth floor. There were two doors, labeled B and C, that were situated in the right place. He rang B's doorbell, waited a few seconds, then rang again. After a brief pause, a childish voice answered from the other side of the door: Who is it? It was the voice of a boy who was probably in his early teens. Sorry, wrong room, Roberto said. He waited a minute and went over to door C, where he rang the bell and knocked several times without any answer. He went down to the third floor and this time began with door C, switching the order, but with the same result as at the previous door C. There was no one home. Then, as he was about to knock on the other door, it suddenly opened and a man with several days' worth of beard and a worn-out coat came out, darted a look at Roberto, then looked at the floor and walked briskly off down the stairs. When somebody behind the door began to shut it, Roberto stepped forward to hold it open. Wait, please, he said. The person on the other side, whom he couldn't see, pushed harder, and finally closed the door. Roberto rang the doorbell, waited a few seconds that went on and on, then heard a woman's voice:

"What do you want?"

"I'm looking for a woman who lives in this building, a black girl . . . it's something important," he said.

"She's gone, she's not here anymore," said the woman's voice on the other side.

"She's gone?"

"Yep," she said. And then she asked, "Why were you shoving on the door? Are you drunk?"

"No, sorry."

"You got money?"

"Yeah," said Roberto. He took his wallet out of his pocket, found a fifty-euro bill, and held it in front of the peephole.

The door opened, but Roberto didn't see the woman until he'd already stepped across the threshold. She closed the door. She was a blond with curly hair, who must have been well into her forties, very thin, and had nothing on except an open dressing gown that gave him a look at her black bra and underwear. Come on, she said, and tromped down the hallway in high heels. As Roberto followed her down the same long hallway from his dream, she said:

"Abeba isn't here anymore, but you don't mind, do you, hon? I'm still around, and I'm real good, better than her."

She showed Roberto a bathroom and told him to wash. He went in, closed the door, and looked around at the meager facilities, at the black-and-white floor tiles, like a chessboard, he thought. Then he looked at his face in the small shaving mirror, at his eyes, the brown irises, the pupils, and felt dizzy. He turned on the faucet and splashed some water on his face, then he let the hot stream run over his hands for a while, until a knock on the door jolted him out of his daydreaming. Coming, he said, turning off the faucet. He washed his groin in the bidet and dried himself with toilet paper.

When he walked into the room, she was lying on the bed, naked except for a pair of black stockings pulled up over her long white legs. He took off his clothes and lay down next to her. He looked around the room, it was the same as the room in his dream, the curtains were drawn shut over the same window. He stared at the stain-covered walls, then at the floor, then he looked from his naked body on the bed to the woman's hands, nothing like the black, long-fingered hands of the woman in his dream. Her fingers were stubs ending in jagged nails whose dark-red polish was chipped away.

"Sweetie, baby," she whispered as she ran her hands and lips over his body. He gently gripped her shoulder: "Wait," he said, "I need to know where the black girl is."

"Abeba? She's gone, she's not here anymore, really, I don't know, and if I did, I wouldn't tell you, either, just like I didn't tell that cop. What do I care where she is? It's none of my business."

Roberto repeated the name in his head—Abeba—and lay there thinking about what the woman had said. He wanted to ask her about the cop who'd been there, but he didn't say anything. Her fingers were stroking his penis. Then she slid down until her face was in front of his crotch.

Roberto felt her saliva on his skin, he could smell it. He clamped his eyes shut as hard as he could, drifting away from the room, from the smell so much like the smell in his dream, drifting away from that hooker, drifting away from his dream, from Abeba, from the blood in his dream, from the guts in his dream. His eyes were still clamped shut when, after slipping a condom on him, she swung a leg over and he was in. He closed his eyes and pictured a woman with white skin and black hair. He imagined the thin, elastic body of Paula above him.

Not far away from that place, Jacobo was lying next to the thin, glistening, black body of another woman. He ran his hand up a long thigh, over her waist, and up to her chest, trying to catch his breath. She was staring at him.

"You don't have family here?" Jacobo asked.

"No," she said.

"You don't have anybody?"

"I had a husband."

"But not anymore?"

"He's dead."

Jacobo, after a silence, hesitating to ask any more questions, finally did:

"Did he die back in Ethiopia?"

"No, he died here, I know it. It happened after we separated."

"Separated?"

"Yes, we separated because of our son. My husband didn't want to be there when our son was born, he wasn't meant to be born anywhere near him, because our son is carrying the *seed* inside him, and my husband didn't put that seed inside me because he's clean. It's in him. My husband knew it, and so do I."

"So . . . why do you say your husband's dead? How do you know?"

"I know. They've killed him somewhere . . . nearby, just a little while ago. He almost got to find what he was looking for, but they killed him."

"Killed him!" he said. And then after a pause: "What was he looking for?"

"Me, our son. He'd give up anything for us, his honor included. But he decided on that after," she said and fell silent. She turned onto her back in the small bed and lay there, staring at the ceiling.

It was only after some time had passed that, as she stroked the slight bulge in her stomach, she added:

"He was going to come here and save us."

7.

I have always had the impression that we were close, like two pieces of fruit from the same branch. Day is dawning as I write to you, thunder rumbles faintly; today it will rain. I imagine you rising in your bed. That anguish you feel, I feel it too, Roberto read. He closed the book and was left gazing at the infinite, as they write in novels, but actually he was gazing at somewhere else, far away, which is what really happens, because the infinite, its comprehension or the thought of it, is beyond the reach of man.

Whatever by Michel Houellebecq rested in his lap. Roberto was having trouble believing what he'd just read in the online edition of a local newspaper. On Saturday, a mere two days from then, Michel Houellebecq would be in Antas, a town in the Almerían Levant a quick sixty miles from the capital of the province. He had read that the French writer would be there due to a series of coincidences, and would be reading poems from his latest book coming out from his Spanish publisher—an omnibus edition of his four poetry collections. It struck him as incredibly bizarre, unreal, and almost unbelievable that the famous French author, the most recent winner of the Prix Goncourt, just so happened to be going to Antas to give a reading.

Roberto's first encounter with this author's work happened years ago with his novel *The Elementary Particles*, which Roberto left unfinished, having been disgusted by the author's crude, offhand treatment of certain lurid episodes in the lives of the two main characters, who were half-brothers. He went a year without opening the book again, until one scorching summer afternoon, overwhelmed by the suffocating heat, cold beer in hand, Roberto's eyes came to rest on, or rather, collided with (to use another, more exact phrase) the book on its shelf. From then on, the Frenchman would have a deep impact on him and would influence not only the way he appreciated literature but also the way he saw life, even the way he wrote and turned events into fiction in his first pieces of writing. He went on to read *Platform, Whatever, The Possibility of an Island*—a book he stood in awe of—and *The Map and the Territory*.

That same day, Paula had informed him over the phone that she would be taking a bus down from Madrid on Saturday. The first thing Roberto had done after finding out about Houellebecq was to, in turn, call her and see if she could change the date of her ticket—to a day earlier, if possible—so he could see her the night she got in and have a relaxed chat over dinner. Then, Saturday, if she liked, she could come along with them to the reading. Like the other times, Paula's deliberate voice lingering on the consonants flustered him, putting him in a state between excitement and doubt. She said that changing the ticket wouldn't be a problem. When Roberto got off the phone with her, he called Jacobo and told him the plan. It was agreed that the three of them would go out to dinner on Friday after Paula had arrived in Almería and taken some time to rest in the hotel. He also said he'd handle calling to change the reservation to tomorrow. On Saturday, they'd go to Antas for the Houellebecq reading, which Paula also seemed excited about attending. Once there, he assumed they wouldn't have any problems finding a cheap hotel to sleep in or else they could just drive back home that night.

After she hung up, Paula sat and thought about the oddness of all that had occurred over the past few days, she thought about *the incident*—her private term for what had happened at the boardinghouse—thought about the first, extremely bizarre conversation she'd had with Roberto, who'd been on the other end of the line when she'd been expecting to hear the voice of her uncle, about the subsequent conversations with Roberto concerning her book, conversations that began abruptly, were full of indecisive pauses that Paula didn't quite know how to interpret, and ended just as suddenly as they'd begun. And now she had to move her trip up a day sooner, because this man, who it seemed was going to be her publisher, wanted to go to a Michel Houellebecq reading in a small, out-of-the-way town in the Almerían Levant.

Paula took mental stock of what little money she still had. She'd checked out of the boardinghouse where *the incident* had occurred, losing two nights' worth of her advance payment, which the boardinghouse owner refused to reimburse. She'd been compelled to find another boardinghouse, even cheaper, dirtier, and grimmer than the last. She'd also bought the bus ticket that she was hoping she could exchange without getting charged an extra fee. Now she was left with basically nothing.

The bus ride began comfortably, and Paula spent the first part of the trip watching the landscape change from urban to industrial to the Madrid suburbs, full of housing developments and large business parks, and these in turn became infinite empty fields that faded into the horizon. The color of the soil, which would suddenly shift from reddish to ocher, fascinated Paula. She imagined the way the red and then the parched ocher soil would feel between her fingers.

Around the halfway mark, in the late afternoon, the bus made a stop at a gas station by a roadside diner at the edge of a small town off the highway.

Paula got down from the bus slowly, being careful not to stumble. Getting off buses always posed a challenge.

She was one of the last to leave. She always tried to wait
like this and not delay the exiting of the other passengers,
who, in this case, were already walking around—stretching
their legs or going into the bar for a drink or to the bathroom. She made her way to the bar. It was a far cry from
clean, and loose wrappers and scraps were strewn along the
floor under the bar top. The walls were covered in shelves
stocked with an assortment of local merchandise, along
with lighters, key fobs, CDs to suit all tastes, and porno
videos. On the wall behind the bar there were framed pictures of soccer teams and a large flag showing the shield of
St. John's eagle with yoke and arrows.

She ordered a café con leche from a skinny waiter in
a white shirt and black pants. When he brought her the
coffee, she carefully gripped the cup and went to one of
the tables by the window looking out on the parking lot.
The cup's heat in her hands felt comforting. She took a few
sips while watching the different sorts of people crowding
the bar. Even though she hadn't had anything to drink in
the last few hours, thinking she'd go the whole trip without needing to use the bathroom, she now felt like she
had to pee, which annoyed her, and she cursed her little
slip-up. She had already lost a lot of time on the coffee,
and it would be no treat to go through the awkward task
of removing her prosthetic leg to pee and then putting it
back on again in the bathroom—sure to be a pigsty—of
a roadside bar. As she was heading for the bathroom, she
saw the door close behind a fat woman in spandex clothes
that emphasized her obesity. So she waited for several minutes outside the door, wondering how long it would take.
What the hell is that woman doing in there? she thought.
She gave a start when the woman suddenly emerged. She
hadn't heard the sound of the toilet flushing. The woman,

unexpectedly finding Paula there, looked her in the eye for a moment, and then immediately averted her gaze. Paula moved slowly out of the woman's way, and the stinking air hit her in the face. She felt like holding it in, but thinking there probably wouldn't be any more stops she decided to use the bathroom. When she closed the door and turned on the light she saw that the floor was covered in piss. She flushed the toilet and carefully cleaned the seat with toilet paper. Putting her cane aside and leaning her body against the wall, she began to unfasten the straps of her prosthetic leg. She sat down on the toilet paper she'd arranged on the seat. As she was standing back up, she reached out to the wall for support, and her fingers slipped on the wet tiles, throwing her off balance and onto the piss-soaked floor, spraining an arm. When she breathed in, the smell of the floor made her gag. With tears in her eyes she managed to get up. Her clothes and hair were covered in filth and wet with urine. She retched again and was barely able to keep down the vomit. Crying now, she managed to put her prosthetic leg back on. She washed her face and arms as well as she could, checked that her aching elbow was more or less all right, and left.

As soon as she stepped out of the restroom, she looked out the window onto the parking lot and realized the bus was no longer there. She went back to her table, containing the urge to burst into tears. She sat down and stared at her cup of coffee, from which she'd barely even drunk a mouthful. She remained there for a while, until the red dusk gave way to darkness. Then she thought to herself that she had to do something. She didn't have any money to call a taxi or to find a hotel and try catching another bus in the morning. She considered that the best thing would be to call Roberto and explain the situation, but she hadn't even

met him in person yet, she thought, so how would she
explain all this? It was then she noticed a man sitting at a
table by the door. After a few seconds she recognized him.
He was one of the passengers from the bus. And he was the
same man she'd bumped into once in the hallway of the
boardinghouse where she'd been staying. She remembered
now. She remembered the way he'd stared at her, as if he
knew her, or rather, as if he sensed he knew her but didn't
know for sure. When she looked at him, the man looked
down at his cell phone lying on the table, as if addressing
missed calls or texts.

Paula sat there for a while, staring at him without caring if he noticed. This small town must be his final stop,
she thought, but she found it strange that the man might
have any reason to travel there. He was tall and thin, fiftysomething, with an abundance of curly hair and a five
o'clock shadow covering his cheeks. He had on brown trou-
sers and a dark coat, and under the table she could make
out a pair of spotless leather moccasins. Although his clothes
were expensive, there was a certain abandon in the way
they'd been thrown on his body, a certain disarray, a certain
neglect, as if it didn't really matter how they fit, or as if it
used to matter, but not anymore. There was a sadness to
it, thought Paula. Then the idea that this man had stayed
in the same boardinghouse as she'd stayed in, and also just
so happened to take the same bus, struck her as unlikely
to be coincidental.

Paula was frightened, or at least on alert, but she con-
sciously pushed the feeling out of her mind. Then, having
decided what to do, she rose from the table and walked
right up to him, asking if she could sit down. Without
waiting for an answer, she took a seat and told him that
she knew he'd been watching her and that he'd ridden the

same bus, she'd noticed him in passing, she remembered him. She said she'd noticed his watch, his silver-plated vintage watch, adding that she liked vintage watches and men who wore vintage watches like the one on his wrist, and men who wore leather moccasins, too. He was about to say something, but she put her finger to her lips, and he remained quiet. She told him to let her talk first because if she didn't say everything she wanted to say right now, she'd lose her nerve. She told him she'd missed the bus and didn't have any money, and said that if he wanted, in exchange for a bit of cash for a hotel room and another bus ticket, he could go to bed with her.

They were walking along a sparsely lit street. Some of the lamps barely gave off any light, the others were completely done for.

"My name's Paula," she said.

"I'm Marcelo," the man said, and seemed to hesitate for a moment over whether to shake her hand, which in the end he did. She could be my daughter, Marcelo thought, the daughter I could've had with Luisa, but didn't, and he continued to match his pace to hers, which was slow, and somehow unusual. As he watched the way she walked, throwing her weight on the cane after each step, Marcelo wondered what defect in her legs might be forcing her to hobble like this and use a cane.

They checked in at the only hotel in town. Marcelo paid cash. There was only one bed in the room, a double, and behind a wooden door painted brown and falling off its hinges there was a tiny bathroom with a shower.

"If you don't mind, when we're done, I'll sleep here too," Marcelo said.

"Whatever you want," she said.

"I'm going to step into the bathroom for a second, then you can go in if you want to wash up," he said.

"Sure, I need to take a shower. I stink," Paula said.

To a certain degree, Marcelo thought, this was true, when walking with her he had noticed the unpleasant odor.

When it was her turn to use the bathroom, she said she'd be a little while, since she had to both shower and wash her clothes. She asked him whether he'd mind if she left her clothes to dry on the shower rod.

"Of course not," Marcelo answered, his eyes following her to the bathroom door. Then he turned on the TV, put it on mute, and occupied himself by flipping channels, while listening to the sound of falling water coming from the bathroom. He lay on the bed like this for a while, feeling sleepy and nodding off, bored by all the junk on TV. He regretted not having a book with him. Just as he was closing his eyes, he heard the bathroom door open, and, as if in a vision, Marcelo thought, or as if he were dreaming, or maybe dead and in hell, from a cloud of steam he saw a nude one-legged woman appear, like some kind of monster, leaning on the doorjamb.

"Give me a hand, please," she said.

Startled out of his drowsiness by the sight, he went over to the girl, and as he stood beside her, holding her by the arm, he saw her cane leaning against the tiled wall and the other leg made of metal and plastic lying across the sink, like the leg of a life-sized doll mutilated by a gigantic child in some cruel game.

She leaned on him, and they went to the bed, where he helped her sit down. She dragged herself on her back up to the pillows, using her hands, her leg, and the stump that protruded a short way from her groin. She propped herself on her elbows and stared at him.

He saw something in her eyes he couldn't quite decipher, as if she were looking out at him from another time, from the future, and then he was struck by the notion that the eyes staring at him belonged to the future but were watching him from the present, and the present in which those hard eyes were staring at him seemed like the past—they were eyes that would have already seen him die, that had seen him buried in a future cemetery, in a cemetery surrounded by mountains of trash, where starving dogs and children were scavenging, eyes that had seen him buried in an apocalyptic era in the apocalyptic cemetery of a world that was also apocalyptic, and which now was not—which now would not be—his world. And then she spread her one leg and her stump of pink skin, showing her cunt, and said:

"So, Marcelo . . . are you going to fuck me?"

THE PART ABOUT MARCELO

1.

Marcelo Plaza discovered Paula Boccia's work before Roberto Fate did, but under different circumstances. It happened on a vacation he took with his wife, Luisa, to Buenos Aires, during the summer of 2012. Refusing to take no for an answer, she had managed to convince him to take the trip all the way across the Atlantic. Maybe Luisa thought it would reunite them, give them back the feeling of being alone, far away from the daily routine, where they'd recuperate something that she sensed hadn't died yet, or was only sleeping. It was their last trip together. Three months later, they separated.

One gray August morning, after drinking a cup of coffee and dialing Luisa's cell phone three times, finding it off each time, Marcelo went out for a walk to pass the time and wait for her to come back. Maybe he'd been too hard on her earlier, maybe it was stupid to argue about something so trivial, but those details, those little differences, always seemed to conceal something bigger, something far more important, something that remained hidden.

Deep in thought, he headed down Avenida de Mayo, in case he might run into her there. He wandered around for a long time before ducking into a small bookstore for distraction. As he was browsing the shelves, the title on a spine caught his eye. He took the book from the shelf. The cover art was Titian's painting *Venus with a Mirror*. The book was called *Skins* and it was by a Paula Boccia. He read the back cover and then opened to a random page and scanned through a few passages.

Marcelo bought the book and returned to the hotel. Luisa was still not back. He went through the minibar and decided on small bottle of whiskey, which he mixed with a splash of water. The book he'd bought impulsively, because of the title and the image on the cover, lay on the bedside table. He'd always liked that painting by Titian—the one of Venus contemplating herself in a mirror held up by her son Cupid, the god of love—and considered it the best rendition by any painter of this theme from myth, setting a precedent that not even Velázquez or Rubens had outperformed.

I should go and get something to eat, Marcelo thought, but he didn't feel hungry, so he decided to lie back in bed and read a bit while he waited for Luisa. Taking sips from his glass of whiskey, he began to read *Skins*. It opened with an epigraph by Alfred Victor de Vigny: "Man is an apprentice and pain is his master." The novel was then divided into two parts. The first part told the story of a trip that a middle-aged couple of quite comfortable means took to Venice, which was modeled on the trip taken in 1869 by the writer Leopold von Sacher-Masoch—from whose last name, Marcelo later learned, the word *masochism* was derived. They departed from Lviv, formerly Lemberg,

where the writer was originally from, after signing a submission contract like the one Sacher-Masoch had signed
with Fanny Pistor, his lover. The married couple, both
cultured people, had discovered Sacher-Masoch's semiau-
tobiographical novel *Venus in Furs* and been hypnotized
by its sensuality, but also by the search for emotions that
the main character undertook, in which pain is a bridge to
pleasure, and by the search, too, for a justification of one's
own existence by submission to someone else, a superior
other. In Paula Boccia's novel, the couple's getaway that
began as an experiment, an extravagance they might allow
themselves so they could escape their routine and dabble
in sexual adventures, ended in the marriage's breakup. One
night, while they were engaged in intercourse after arriving
in Venice, the wife carried the role of mistress to its fur-
thest consequences, using infidelity as the greatest punish-
ment of the submissive—as in Sacher-Masoch's book. This
was something they had laughed and cracked jokes about
while planning the trip, something that never would have
even crossed their minds. That night when he was in bed
with her, somebody knocked on the bedroom door. To his
great surprise, she got up, showing no surprise herself at
this untimely visit, and with nothing on but leather stiletto
boots, she opened the door to a man dressed in black who
was wearing a Venetian carnival mask and let him in. She
ordered her husband to be silent and watch, and as her
bewildered spouse looked on, she kneeled down in front
of the other man and began to unzip his fly.

Then the reader is given an account of the husband's
desperate and aimless flight through the dark streets of
Venice in a night that seemed to have no end.

The second part began with the following quote from
the Velvet Underground:

Your servant comes in bells, please don't forsake him.
Strike, dear Mistress, and cure his heart.

From this point on—with the feeling that the Velvet Underground's song "Venus in Furs" is always somehow present—the book launches into the description of a wave of violent crimes that take place in Venice. All the victims are found dead and show evidence of having been forced into some form of sexual submission. A policeman in his last year before retirement investigates the deaths, but only seems to be getting further and further away from the killer. He also seems to be getting further and further away from reality, coming to justify the murders, even sympathizing with the killer. The book ends with a series of reflections by the policeman on the victims' skin and his own. This takes place beneath the yellow light of a large lamp, in a room covered in rugs, in the center of which, lying motionless on a bed, is a naked man whose hands are cuffed behind his back. The white sheets are disarranged and stained a dark ocher. In this scene, described in minute detail, the old policeman mechanically pets the man's back, staring, meanwhile, at the greenish stains on the wall. Then he lies down next to him, face to face with the corpse. He looks at its contorted features. On its closed lips, a viscous, dull-white liquid still hasn't dried. Then, under his breath, the policeman delivers the novel's last sentence: *In the end, the damp rots everything.*

2.

Back in Madrid, they were strange days for Marcelo. One Sunday morning, he told his wife it was over. Luisa first reacted with rage, lashing out and making threats, then, confronted with Marcelo's impassive stare, she begged him not to leave her. Having exhausted her tears, she ended her plea with a long, bitter monologue on the children they'd never had, the time wasted, and everything she'd given up doing and having just to stick with him all these years.

Two days later Marcelo moved into a rented studio apartment, bringing only a few things: the clothes he wore most often, some toiletries, and three CDs—one by Portishead, another by the composer György Ligeti, and the album *10,000 Days* by Tool, which he listened to on a loop throughout the first day he spent confined to his small new apartment.

The following morning, he called the office where he worked and said he felt sick and wouldn't be coming in that day, adding that he might be out tomorrow as well. What he didn't say was that he had no intention of going back to the office ever again, that this path he was setting out on was a path with no return, and he scarcely knew how it would end. Then, he went down to the street with an empty bottle and the Portishead CD. He threw the bottle in the nearest recycling container and gave the CD to the first person whose path he crossed.

Marcelo transferred the Tool CD to an iPod he hardly ever took a break from in the following days, other than to reread the same handful of passages from Paula Boccia's book, which always seemed to be in reach. He bought some clothes—sportswear, more or less, something comfortable for walking in—and a new pair of leather moccasins, and started to go out on long walks, never unaccompanied by his iPod. For entire afternoons, he'd wander through streets and neighborhoods he barely knew, taking it all in while listening to the music playing nonstop in his headphones.

Very early one morning, before the sun had risen, he was walking in a neighborhood on the edge of town where he'd never been. Turning the corner of a newer, well-lit avenue, he came onto a street that was almost entirely dark, where, as he passed by a cluster of overflowing garbage containers, he was hit with the rancid stink of decomposing matter. Next to the containers was a pile of torn garbage bags, and he supposed some dog had been through them because trash was strewn all around. Then something moved, he just caught a glimpse of it out of the corner of his eye. Marcelo turned around and stood there for a few minutes, watching the containers and the surrounding debris. The dawn light began to lengthen the shadows cast by the food scraps and various discarded objects scattered across the pavement, lending them an unreal quality. Then something stirred again. Marcelo focused his eyes, then focused them more, until the outlines of things started to blur. Then they looked much closer, and as a matter of fact they were—he wondered how he'd drawn so close to them. He didn't remember having done so, he thought, surprised. Then something stirred again, and from the waste and scraps of rotting food a hand emerged, then a hand that transformed into a filthy arm with pasty skin, culminating in a hand whose fingers kept moving as if trying to grab something in the air, something that didn't exist or that Marcelo simply couldn't see. And Marcelo knelt by the refuse and litter, he knelt by the rotting waste, he knelt in front of the arm protruding from the heap of junk, he knelt and cried, cried for all this beauty and ugliness, and for this arm—which in some way could have been, or actually was, his own.

At some point, he got up and started walking around this

unfamiliar part of the city. He wandered aimlessly for a long time, until he began to come across streets that he vaguely recognized, and in the end he was able to find his way back to his small apartment.

He returned to this place several times. The first time was in the morning, and aside from the sun that was already high above him, he didn't see anything or anyone there. He went back very late the following night, so late it was almost morning, and found a garbage truck lifting the containers with its mechanical arm and emptying them into the back of the truck. He saw the sanitation workers curse and complain as they looked at the scraps and cardboard littering the ground, but none of them seemed to have the least intention of clearing any of it away.

The third time he returned to the alley, it was late evening. He spotted the man there, by the containers. The man was sitting on the curb. His tattered clothes seemed to have been hung from his body rather than put there to dress it. A long, unkempt beard covered his face of indeterminate age, a face that could have belonged to a twentysomething just as easily as to a man of sixty. Standing at a distance and observing him, Marcelo noticed that whenever somebody came up and threw a bag of trash inside a container, the man would take it out, rip it open, and scatter its contents on the ground. Then, with hands that looked less like hands than like the paws of some animal, a sick, old animal, he'd rummage through the debris. Sometimes it looked as though he'd found something, and then his eyes would light up and he'd look left and right, as if he were afraid somebody was going to come and take away his newfound treasure.

Every evening, Marcelo would return to the alley to

observe the beggar. He'd stay there for a long time, watching, following the beggar to the entrance of a supermarket, where he would sit down and beg, putting a cardboard box by his side, into which, now and then, somebody, usually an older woman, would toss spare change.

One evening, when Marcelo arrived, he didn't see the beggar anywhere. He went over to the containers, and all of a sudden the beggar's face sprung out from behind one of them, and in a second, was only a few inches from his own. The stench wafting from his skin and breath hit Marcelo like a punch—he felt nauseated.

"Nietzsche is a son of a bitch," the bum said.

"Nietzsche is a son of a bitch," he repeated.

"What?" Marcelo said, unable to understand anything the beggar was saying.

The beggar slowly repeated the philosopher's name, placing a long pause between the syllables: "Nietz-sche," and then he shouted, "is a son of a bitch!"

The fourth time he returned to the alley, it was night. He saw the vagabond sitting on the curb, his mouth moving in silence, counting out coins he took from the cardboard box and sorting them into small heaps on the ground. Then his wrinkled face—more wrinkled than usual because of the spell of concentration he seemed to be under—relaxed into a smile. He put the coins in his worn jacket pocket, got up and began to walk toward Marcelo. Marcelo stood his ground as the man approached, but just as he thought the beggar was going to stop and speak, he brushed past Marcelo as if he'd never seen him before or as if he didn't exist, as if Marcelo were nothing but a spirit or a ghost or both, if there's any difference.

Marcelo followed him for a while down streets that went through relatively new neighborhoods, but were still poorly lit and rather narrow. The beggar turned down a cobbled sidestreet that didn't seem to belong to the surrounding neighborhood. As the two of them approached the entrance of a nightclub, its tinted glass doors swung open and two men emerged and turned to look at them. As Marcelo walked past them, they had cigarettes in their mouths. One of the men glared at him. Up ahead, the street took another right turn, behind which Marcelo lost sight of the beggar, so he picked up his pace, and when he rounded the corner, he saw the beggar approaching somebody leaning against a wall under an arcade. The two figures stood in the shadows, and the other's silhouette looked like that of a fairly young boy. Marcelo walked toward them, stopping a few yards off. The boy turned his head and scrutinized Marcelo from head to toe. He didn't look any more than twenty years old, with dark, close-cropped hair and a tight, black sweater that accentuated his slim build. The beggar, who didn't seem to have noticed Marcelo, or who, if he had, was ignoring him, continued talking with the boy, who stared at him with an apparently amused grimace. The beggar inched closer to the boy, as if he was frightened or trying not to spook him, and placed at the boy's feet the coins he'd taken from his pocket and had been clutching in his hand. Without taking his eyes off the beggar, the boy squatted and picked up the coins, he then took his time counting them across from the beggar's nervous and impatient gaze, and finally stuffed them in a pocket of his jeans. Marcelo witnessed an enormous smile spread across the beggar's face. He watched as the beggar got on his knees and scraped them along the ground toward the boy, until his face was nearly touching the other's groin, and Marcelo also noticed the look of disgust on the boy's face as he began to unzip his fly, but then in one quick, precise, springlike movement his fist traced a perfect arc and struck the beggar in the head, knocking him to the ground. After he got up on all fours, blood started gushing from his mouth and nose, running down his filthy beard and rags. He crawled away like a beaten dog, before scrambling to his feet and running off, brushing past Marcelo. And the boy watched him go.

Then he turned his eyes on Marcelo, who, in turn, stood and stared back.

Unperturbed, the boy simply began to walk away, and Marcelo, without thinking twice, followed him, keeping the same distance. It looked as if the boy was playing a game, zigzagging around the columns of the arcades, pulling ahead in a burst of speed and then slowing down. Sometimes, Marcelo lost sight of him, only to find him again. He'd lost track of the boy around a bend in the road, when, passing a column, he found himself face-to-face with him. The boy had been waiting for him. He had big green eyes and a few freckles on his pale cheeks, which gave him a childish air. His bored expression clashed with his features.

"Give me twenty euros," the boy said.

Confused, Marcelo searched his pockets, found his wallet, and handed him a bill, which the boy deftly put in his jeans—with the beggar's coins, Marcelo thought—without even giving it a glance. Then he got on his knees, unbuttoned Marcelo's pants, pulled down his underwear, and wrapped his fingers around Marcelo's penis. Marcelo grabbed the boy's head and drew it toward his groin. At first, the boy put up some resistance, grabbing Marcelo's thighs and trying to push his head back, but Marcelo didn't let him and pulled his head down even harder. After some gagging, the boy finally gave in, and, feeling his limp body no longer offer the slightest opposition, Marcelo convulsed and ejaculated deep in the boy's throat.

Afterward, Marcelo let go of the boy's head and waited a few seconds for him, still kneeling on the ground, to recuperate. Marcelo handed him another twenty-euro bill, which the boy accepted with tears in his eyes. And that was how, in a wild rage at fifty-two, Marcelo had his first homosexual experience.

From that moment on, a relationship developed between Marcelo and the boy, based on an initial series of sporadic sexual encounters, always quick and brutal, after which Marcelo would give him money.

The boy lived with another man, who was much older, in the man's apartment. According to the boy, the man acted as his boyfriend, and according to Marcelo, as his pimp. And from what he heard, Marcelo gathered that he was also a drug dealer.

A month after they met—while his considerably large bank account was rapidly dwindling from the lack of any income—Marcelo paid for a room in a cheap boarding-house in the city center, so the boy could get away from his pimp and be permanently available. Now Marcelo could go see him whenever he wanted. The boardinghouse was a calm place, and in the hallway Marcelo would only now and then bump into a mute Romanian or a lame girl who used a cane. Only later did the features of this girl with a cane remind him of the features pictured on the back flap of a book.

Sometimes they'd spend the entire day talking about nothing. And while the boy's mind was too childish to maintain intelligent conversations, Marcelo was ultimately attracted to this simplicity and innocence, and to his resigned attitude toward life or what he thought was life. And so he could spend hours talking with the boy about the most trivial things. At such times, after long talks in the always-unmade bed, they would fuck like animals. At other times, they would just fuck.

One day, after Marcelo had made extremely brutal use of him, the boy accused Marcelo of always being rough during sex, and said that a relationship needed another kind of sex, too, that there had to be some tenderness now and then, not just savage fucking. Then the boy fell silent for a moment and stared at the floor, as if he was replaying his own words in his head and thinking them over, and then he looked back at Marcelo, who was still standing in front of him, with his penis now flaccid, and his long, lanky body looking much younger than his fifty-two years, and the boy told him they were a couple, and then, after some hesitation, he said it again, but it sounded like he wasn't so much telling Marcelo as asking him. Then the boy said:

"Because I . . . I . . . I love you."

"Love doesn't exist," Marcelo snapped, and this statement was like the verdict of a judge. The boy felt as if the air in the room had become much thicker, as if it were rancid.

"I love you," the boy said again, but he seemed to say it out of inertia, because he felt sick, as if something had happened, something horrible, something that had affected him enough to make his head spin, something like staring at somebody who's been run over and left for dead on the street, something like staring at a pig hanging in the slaughterhouse, split wide open. Then he added:

"Because you love me, too . . . don't you?" And as soon as he said it, as soon as he asked himself the same thing just after saying it, he knew this feeling of nausea was a premonition of something horrible, and then, in addition to nausea, he felt fear.

It was then that Marcelo spoke, in a mechanical voice, a voice that seemed like it belonged to somebody else while remaining his own, but toneless and without inflection:

"Love does not exist, only possession exists, instinct, the instinct of perpetuation, the instinct of protection, of saving the species, of procreating, of procreating or deciding not to, but that means you're sick, sick like you and me. I'm going to show you that love does not exist and never did, and that I don't love you and never could. I will never be capable of love, and what you think of as love is just self-deception, because you think you can save yourself. You can't love. You can't and neither can I." And taking the leather belt from his pants that lay crumpled on a chair, folding it into his palm, and gripping it so the metal buckle swung loose, he said, "Because someone who loves, could they do what I'm about to do to you?"

THE PART ABOUT THE
DROWNINGS IN THE DESERT

1.

Just two months before a car on Avenida Álvarez Jonte, in Buenos Aires ran over a fourteen-year-old girl named Paula Boccia, who was rushed to the emergency room where she lost a leg, Roberto—now done with his university studies and coming off a string of relationships all marked by the same disillusioned end—married a tall blond girl, a few years younger than himself.

Her name was Cristina, and he'd met her through common friends at a New Year's Eve party. She was tall and thin, with skinny, even somewhat bony legs. By character she was temperamental, and often she was hard to be around, but there were times of overflowing love and affection. Roberto married her when they'd been together only five months, after coming out the other side of a severe depression. Maybe he owed his recovery to the psychiatric treatment he'd undergone, but really, he'd always known— and it was the reason for everything—that he owed it to Cristina.

During that depression, for the second time in his life, Roberto had wanted to die. The first time came when he was just a boy. Then, as later, he would clamp his eyes shut, breathe deeply, and think of a deserted, rocky beach in winter, and of a woman's lukewarm hand, and this is what saved him. Then came Cristina's scrawny, lukewarm hand on his forehead.

After that he married her, intending to lead a peaceful life without surprises. He tried to understand his wife, who was so different from himself, with such different interests, all of them far removed from the love of reading that Roberto had always harbored—and that had only deepened since his adolescence. While there were continual flare-ups between them, they both had stable jobs and certain common objectives, almost all of a material kind, and this helped strike a balance in their marital existence.

In effect, they led separate lives, and while she spent her free time shopping or drinking coffee with some friends—not many—Roberto read Somerset Maugham, André Gide, Chekhov, Yevgeny Zamyatin, Monterroso, Ballard, Ray Bradbury, Bernhard, Hardy, Hemingway, Borges, Sebald, Mann, and Carver. He read a strange novel by Felipe Hernández that he found disturbing. He read Sábato, Valente, Justo Navarro, Alan Pauls, Coetzee, Roth, Houellebecq, Vila-Matas, Ford, Huxley, Céline, Walser, Gombrowicz, Bolaño—more than anyone, Bolaño. He read the apocalyptic, claustrophobic, and only novel by the illustrator Alfred Kubin, a friend of Kafka's, which he wrote during a creative crisis and then illustrated himself. He also read Alejandra Pizarnik, Nicanor Parra, Lorca, and Panero, whom at first he considered a mere lunatic, only to later think he'd been wrong, and that he was in the presence of a genius, only to once again change his mind and consider him a lunatic again, but a genius all the same. He read many others, others whom he forgot quickly, and in anger. Because just as one can hate in anger, strike out, labor, look back, or weep in anger, one can also forget in anger. There are those who try to forget in the purest anger, on the largest scale, but can't, and then only the anger remains—nothing else. Primo Levi was such a person. He could never forget Auschwitz.

As for their sexual relationship, it could be said that this was a link of common consent for the pair, since it was satisfying for both, and these two people who seemed so different and between whom it seemed there could be no understanding or companionship, would mutate into two beings who wanted each other in bed.

After a year together, Cristina became pregnant. And while, to her mind, the pregnancy was a cause for celebration, it filled Roberto with doubts and regrets. So when she started bleeding one morning, a month and a half into her pregnancy, and they confirmed in the hospital that she'd had a miscarriage, he couldn't avoid feeling a relief that later turned against him, until he came to see himself as a total monster. This feeling of guilt, combined with sharp remorse and his secret debt to Cristina for having helped him out of his depression, drove him to bend over backward for his wife from that day on. He took great pains to do everything in his power to help her through this difficult time, which had left her psychically drained.

He tried to be understanding, affectionate, and patient with her. He encouraged her to go out with her friends, and when Cristina refused to leave the house, he persuaded one of them, the one he considered the closest, to pay her regular visits.

The initial coffee chats with this silent Cristina, who looked so out of place, gave way at Roberto's suggestion of eclectic movie nights. These showings were normally scheduled for Thursday evenings and attended by Cristina's two or three best friends.

One evening, after he'd come home from work and before he'd gone to take a shower and then read in bed, he went into the living room, where Cristina was joined in one of these showings by a friend and another girl he didn't know who looked much younger than the other two.

After a brief, friendly greeting, he went to the master bathroom. He closed the door, rolled up his sleeves, turned on the tap, and washed his face at the sink. He looked at himself in the mirror as the water ran down the drain. He thought he noticed a long hair on his upper lip, he looked closer, moving his face closer to the mirror. It wasn't just one hair, there were several—long and black. He wondered how on earth he'd managed to miss them that morning and the one before, because hairs like these didn't spring up in a day. He decided that he had to take better care of himself, be more scrupulous in his morning routine. The steam began to fog up the mirror, and his reflection changed into a mere silhouette. The last clear part of his face that he saw was his right cheek and his upper lip with the black hairs. Like a rat's whiskers, he said to himself. Then he imagined a rat. A rat slinking home to its rat hole in the sewers, tired from its labors. A rat laborer, or maybe a rat mechanic, or a rat journalist, no, most likely it would be a rat policeman, or better yet, a rat detective. Then he heard a groan, almost a whimper, a clear expression of pain. He imagined a rat being killed on the other side of the closed door, in another room of the rat hole. But they were in the sewers, he remembered, and there weren't any predators there, there were only rats. And a rat never kills another rat. His mind wandered again from his train of thought, he repeated that phrase: A rat never kills another rat. He had read it somewhere, but he couldn't remember where. He heard the rat whimper again, above the sound in the background of what seemed to be a movie. He turned off the tap and left the bathroom. In the living room, he saw the rats. Cristina, one of the rats, was sobbing and hugging her friend, her crying apparently growing more and more inconsolable. The young girl (young rat) remained seated in another armchair in silence. At some point somebody turned off the TV. Cristina said she needed to go to bed, and her friend took her to the bedroom, without releasing her from her tight embrace. Roberto was left alone in the living room with the young woman, listening to the muffled sobs that carried down the hallway and through the closed door.

After a little while, her friend opened the living room door and told Roberto that Cristina needed to rest, and when Roberto made as if to get up and go see her, the friend said:

"Don't. She told me she doesn't want to see you right now." And after standing there for a moment looking at the other, younger woman, as if waiting for her to say something, she finally said, "Well, I'm leaving, she should get some rest and so should you, Roberto," and looked once more at the girl, who was still sitting in the armchair without showing the least sign that she intended to get up. Then the friend said goodbye and headed for the door.

When it closed, Roberto went over to the couch and sat down. The girl was in the armchair on his left. He looked

at her: she must have been twentysomething at most, her
hair was jet black, all the more so in contrast with her
incredibly white skin. Her lipstick was blood red and she
had on too much eye makeup. She was dressed all in black
and had several earrings and a nose ring. Roberto couldn't
imagine what in the world the girl was doing there. It was
almost impossible to believe she was Cristina's friend, even
the most fleeting contact between Cristina and this girl
would have seemed incredible. She and his wife were from
totally different planets. Nor could he imagine what the
girl was waiting around for. Why she didn't leave.

"What were you all watching?" Roberto asked, more to
break the silence that was now making him uncomfortable
than to be polite.

"Some shitty movie. It's not even worth mentioning."

"Oh."

And after a short silence the girl said:

"If you want, I'll tell you a movie. One that *is* worth it."

"Yeah? What's it called?"

"I don't remember the title, or maybe I never knew it
in the first place. Let me think," and she sat there with her
lips half-open and a faraway look in her eyes, as if putting
all her concentration into remembering the title of the
movie. Of her fucking movie, Roberto thought, exhausted
and wishing the girl would just leave, wishing he could go
shower, get in bed, and try to sleep.

It was beginning to grow dark and Roberto thought of
getting up and turning on the ceiling light or at least the
floor lamp by the couch. He thought about it, but didn't
do anything, and the room grew dimmer and dimmer, like
life in old age. Then she began to talk:

"The movie starts with a shot of a bed that you see through a half-open door, in the bed there's a young woman having sex with an older man. Then you see a woman's hand carefully shutting the door. The woman's about sixty, and it's her bedroom door she's closing. It's midmorning and she's just come home. You can tell by the way she's behaving that something made her come back before she was expected. Before that young blond woman had finished caressing her husband and moaning lascivious words. Before he could orgasm. There, in their bed, with the same unchanged sheets, which must have still held the smell of her own sleeping body. Before that woman left her house, before that scene could be erased from what she might know, from what she would see of her particular universe, as if nothing had ever happened. The woman behind the closed door might be contemplating the yellow color of the light filtering through the hallway windowpanes. The walls, on the other hand, are white. The panting and agitated breathing she hears behind the door, which is now shut, don't have a color, that's all they are: sounds. Sounds without color, like the sound when she goes down to the kitchen, the sound of her splitting pills into little pieces, pouring sugar into a glass, then water, and mixing it all with a spoon. And doubt? Does that have a color? What about the temptation to exist? Maybe that's what the woman's thinking, or I imagine that's what she might think. In any case, all this would be a murky white, almost gray. As for the vomit on the countertop that she makes herself throw up after a terrible moment of doubt, this does have a color: it's yellow. Afterward, she leaves the house in her car, stops at the nearest ATM, and takes out all the money that her bank's daily maximum will allow. She leaves the city on a highway that runs through a stretch of desert. To the south, just before the line of the horizon, there's a glimpse of the sea, between this and the highway lie acres of plastic-covered farmland, forming another sea. The sheets of plastic reflect the blinding sun. The woman, who we discover is named Eva, keeps driving for several hours until she turns off the highway and stops at a cheap hotel in a small town. She spends the rest of the day sleeping or trying to sleep. When night falls, she asks the front desk if there's a computer she can use to look for something online. She browses through a few websites, writes down some phone numbers, then leaves. It's a dark night, big storm clouds blanket the sky. Finally, she goes into a rather seedy and rundown pub where there's only a pair of men drinking and talking silently, if that adverb can be used this way, but in any case, that's what she thought: They're talking silently. She orders a drink and nurses it, now and then taking a little sip. Then she goes back to the hotel. Back in her room, she reaches into her purse for the paper where she'd jotted down the phone numbers and makes a call. She waits, and, after about a half hour, a young man arrives. They introduce themselves and chat a little, just enough. Then he takes his clothes off and hers, too, slowly, running his hands over her the whole time, and he lays her down on the bed. When they finish, you can tell by the expression on her face that she hasn't had an orgasm, and you can also guess from something she says that she won't have one ever again. Be that as it may, she pays him the agreed amount. A deal is a deal. The next morning, she drives back to the city, parks the car near her front door, and sits there for a while with her hands on the wheel. Then she looks at her cell phone, which she'd put on silent:

there are ten missed calls. She leaves it in the car when she gets out. She walks to the port, goes to the west pier, and comes to the point where it juts farthest into the sea. She looks for a few minutes at the dark water, then takes a step over the void. If someone who didn't know her intentions were watching her then, he'd think the woman was trying to walk on water. She falls into the sea and lets the cold waters cover her until she's lost in a descent to the abyss," the girl said.

Roberto looked at her, sprawled there in the armchair. It didn't look like she was budging anytime soon. He didn't want her to either, he thought. The girl sat up a little, unfastened the buckles on her boots, took them off, and rested her stockinged feet on the couch where Roberto was sitting. Then she continued talking:

"That's just part of the movie, then it goes on. The scene changes to a room with floor-to-ceiling windows that look onto a pool. It looks like a restaurant or a café. There are only two men there, sitting in armchairs, and one of them starts telling the other how Stuart Regen, an American movie producer, managed to track down the writer John O'Brien in order to get rights for a film adaptation of his only published novel at the time, *Leaving Las Vegas*. He says that O'Brien didn't seem too happy about it, which the producer found pretty shocking. Then O'Brien told him that he was worried about what kind of adaptation was going to be made of the novel. He didn't want them to change the plot one iota, including the ending. The man, from his armchair in this café whose plate-glass walls look out over a pool, tells the other guy about how the novel is based on O'Brien's own life. He was born to a middle-class family in Ohio. In his teenage years, O'Brien compulsively read John Steinbeck, then he went to college where, at nineteen, he married one of his classmates, Lisa, and that's also when he started to drink. Alcohol, together with photography, literature, and Lisa herself, would turn out to be lifelong passions. At twenty-three, he left with his wife for Los Angeles, where they survived on a series of menial jobs at restaurants and bars. By then he was a confirmed alcoholic. He drank vodka, whiskey, and tequila, and ate almost nothing. There was one year, however, when he managed to stay more or less sober, and during that time he wrote what seems to be his only novel, which was published by a small press in Kansas. Then he went back to drinking and decided that he'd drink forever and ever, that he'd drink himself to death. He separated from his wife, to whom he dedicated his book: *For Lisa, close to the action.* He gave away his library and, in April 1994, at the age of thirty-three, he shot himself in the temple. He didn't leave a suicide note, his novel was enough. There were three months left until the premiere of the film adaptation of *Leaving Las Vegas.*

"Then the man who's talking," the girl continued, "looks through the glass wall at the pool. The camera follows his attention, and the scene shifts to the small poolside garden. There's Nicolas Cage on a deck chair, taking long pulls from a bottle of whiskey while he looks at the large gray storm clouds in the sky. Then Elisabeth Shue enters the scene dressed like a prostitute. She looks up at the sky, murmurs something you don't hear, and lies down on the other deck chair. The camera moves into a close-up of Cage drinking. There's an open book on his lap. The camera zooms in. On the screen there's a sentence you can read perfectly: *Beyond a certain point there is no return. This point has to be reached.* That's when the storm breaks and it starts to pour, and they watch the rain falling on the pool, on the paper of the book, blotting out that sentence, and on the garden grass, and beyond it, falling on the parched desert soil of Las Vegas or California or Almería. *Beyond a certain point there is no return. This point has to be reached,* Elisabeth Shue says. Nicolas Cage nods in agreement. The shot gradually zooms out from the scene, rising up into the rain in the dark sky, but before the main characters' voices lose all possibility of being heard, before they fade away into a speck of nothingness, Nicolas Cage says: "We'll just have to try walking on water."

When she'd said all this, the girl stretched out her legs, grazing Roberto's knees with her feet. He looked at those feet touching him, feeling their pressure.

After a brief silence, Roberto said:

"Well, that's obviously not a real movie. And you didn't just make it up now, either. The whole thing's too elaborate."

"It's late," she said. "I have to go."

She took her feet off him and put her boots back on. Roberto felt a huge emptiness.

Three days later, Cristina left the house.

Two weeks after that, Roberto ran into the girl again at a café, while he was getting a cup of coffee with an acquaintance. She was there with someone too, another girl her age. When Roberto went over to talk with her, the other girl stood off to the side, as if she and the girl from Roberto's weren't together, as if Roberto, by being from another generation, belonged to another species, making any communication impossible.

When they said goodbye, they exchanged phone numbers.

Two nights later, they met at Roberto's house. The girl brought over several videos, which they spent the night watching. The videos were short underground movies and always featured people on the margins of civilization. In one of them, a young man with a beard and a bare torso covered in neo-Nazi tattoos nervously paced back and forth in a miserable room full of graffiti and trash. Then electronic music began to play. Little by little, he began to dance, getting gradually more intense, until his dancing turned into wild flailing. That was it.

In another video, the screen showed a room with a bed on one side and on the opposite side a closed door. The scene looked like it was recorded by a camera fixed in a ceiling corner, in what was apparently a bedroom. Along the bottom right edge of the screen, the shot registered the date and time of the recording. The door opened and a skinny, very skinny young man in his twenties entered the room with a duffel bag. He sat down on the bed and opened the duffel bag and arranged various cans and tubes of paint on the bedsheet. Then he stripped down to his underwear. His ribs and collarbones jutted out from beneath his skin, unadulterated by an ounce of fat. The cans turned out to contain not paint but makeup. Sitting on the bed, he opened them and lathered it on his body and face. His skin now looked much more withered and pale. Then, with some lipstick and another two cans of body paint, one very dark and the other red, he outlined and filled in wounds and sores all over his skin. Then he got into the bed and lay motionless for a few seconds, with his mouth open in a look of pain, and his eyes open, barely blinking, letting the camera record him. Finally, he got up, walked over to the camera, reached out his hand, and, as a close-up of his face was being shot, he turned off the camera.

The second scene was exactly like the first except for two things: although the time was more or less the same, only differing from the previous recording by a few minutes, the date showed it was three weeks later. The other difference lay in the boy's body. It was now monstrously thin. Otherwise, the sequence of actions recorded was the same.

The third and final scene, although it began in the same way, diverged from the previous ones. The recording followed the same temporal ratio: recorded three minutes later, three weeks after the previous scene. And if the boy had been skin and bones before, now he looked like a skeleton coated in a glistening membrane, that apparently was skin. He couldn't even walk upright as he moved around the room. The process of stripping down to his underwear was also clearly more difficult. In this third scene, there was no makeup. There was no need. He lay down in the bed, and after several minutes, he'd managed to stay so still, he'd achieved such dominion over himself, without moving even a single muscle, without blinking, that the viewer couldn't help but feel, aside from horror, a conflicted sense of admiration. After another minute or two of the boy lying motionless in the bed, the door opened and a heavy-built man with a ski mask covering his face walked in, went to the camera, and turned it off.

Several more rendezvous went by in the same way. They always met at Roberto's apartment, where they'd watch videos and then talk about them over beer. And sometimes Roberto would pull down a book from the shelves and read her something. Aside from that first grazing of her feet on his knees, there wasn't the slightest physical contact between them. Except for the fourth time they saw each other, when, in the apartment doorway as she was leaving, she stood up on tiptoe and kissed Roberto on the lips.

"We won't be seeing each other anymore," she said. And she left.

A few days later a message from Cristina, whom he'd heard nothing from since she'd gone, appeared on his cell phone. *Was that little bitch a good fuck?* it said. A week later, the divorce papers arrived in the mail.

2.

There were four fundamental events in Jacobo's life. Four events linked closely to horror, to the contemplation of it, and to its annihilating power, and signaled a turning point in his personality, marked from then on by the awareness of dread.

The first time Jacobo encountered horror up close was in the tenderness of his early childhood, when his parents took him to visit some relatives who lived in a small mountain village, where his father was born and raised. These family members had invited his parents for the celebration of the pig slaughter, and while his parents made sure the little one couldn't see anything at all to do with the animal's killing, Jacobo would remember the pig's wild squeals for the rest of his life. In time, he would unconsciously add to this memory until it included an exact visual scenario of the animal meeting its death. Jacobo, who was barely seven years old, found out for himself, by asking around, how the butcher savagely pierces the animal's jaw with a metal hook and drags it to the wooden bench, where he ties it down with rope, and then stabs it with a knife, piercing the jugular. The blood, gushing out, is collected in buckets, and the animal squeals desperately from the unbearable pain until, after a long time, it bleeds to death. All these images—the result of explanations given to the boy in answer to his many questions—went on reworking his memories. And before long, the memories didn't just consist of the squeals that had lodged themselves forever in his young head—now the images his brain produced were unconsciously and without the least effort synchronized to the sounds he'd heard that day. And so, by the time Jacobo Cruz had turned eight years old, he understood that the brutality of human beings had no limits, and he had no desire to belong to that savage and brutal species. He didn't want to be human. Although he was only a boy, Jacobo wished to have never been born.

The second event that left a decisive mark on Jacobo, defining a part of his personality and igniting a hatred of anything different or unfamiliar, happened in his adolescence. While, as an adult, he was overweight with a persistently receding hairline that indicated alopecia, when he was a teenager and in his prime, Jacobo had played several sports and practiced obsessively, resulting in a muscular, athletic physique.

It happened one summer when he was sixteen, during a night out that lasted until almost morning among the trendy bars near the beach. Toward dawn, he was feeling so sick that he decided to leave his friends and go for a walk on the beach, deserted at that hour. He went down to the shore, took off his T-shirt, and lay down on his back, closing his eyes and feeling immediate relief at the icy touch of wet sand on his skin. He didn't know how much time went by this way, in a kind of waking dream. The contact of a calloused hand on his chest jolted him out of his daze. When he opened his eyes he saw a much older man lying next to him and stroking his chest. What the fuck are you doing? Jacobo said. Startled, the man withdrew his hand. Sorry, he said, I thought you'd seen me come up. I walked up to you and you didn't do anything, I thought you wanted me to make the first move. And when he'd said this, something inside Jacobo snapped, something inside him shifted a little, almost imperceptibly, but forever, and Jacobo sat up and, with an immature but powerful arm, trained on weight-lifting equipment, he grabbed the man by the neck, and as the man looked at him in astonishment, eyes bulging, stammering words of apology, Jacobo raised his right fist and delivered a brutal blow straight to his face. After the first punch came another and another, until the man was lying unconscious on the sand, his face covered in blood. Then, breathing so hard it looked like his chest was going to burst, Jacobo stopped hitting the man and stood still, staring at him. Scared, realizing what he'd done, he checked to make sure the man was breathing. He felt the beginnings of an immense anger at himself, as he realized the man had been confused, that the whole thing had come from a misunderstanding, that this man had thought he was queer. But whatever it was that had snapped inside him turned his thoughts in another direction, and made him lay the blame on this man for being gay, for having touched him, and for having made him do what he'd done. He's the one who's responsible for this, not me, he said to himself. And then Jacobo hated him.

He hated him for being different. Because anything that's different is a threat, he thought.

The third occasion was in his adulthood, the night he'd gone to the Essence nightclub, where Jacobo had opened the bathroom door that the bargirl was pounding on and come face-to-face with pure horror, which upset the precarious balance that, until then, he'd considered stable, and that had reconciled him once more with the human species, to which, over the years, he had come to accept that he belonged.

The fourth time Jacobo encountered horror, it settled in and annihilated everything. Horror descended on him and destroyed what, at that time in his life, he longed for most. It destroyed the woman who, although she was certainly a departure, and even more sad than a departure, was the first and only one for whom Jacobo had felt something, something that, if it wasn't love, was its possibility, its spark, its glow, one of the few surprises in life that steer our fates in another direction and give us hope (happiness? perhaps), something to cling to, at least, something like a long, thin body, a body behind which there was a gleam of love, its possibility. And so there was only a woman's body with a mutilated head, a woman's body sliced open from collarbone to pelvis, like that first time, like a pig, hanging from a metal hook after the slaughter.

Horror, yes. And this time the horror had come to stay, and it annihilated everything.

Horror.

The horror following the 2012 floods in the Almerían Levant and the events of Antas, which Roberto Fate described in a book he wrote called *The Endless Rose*. The horror of the crime detailed in Roberto Fate's novel, which he wrote during the first few months of 2013. At first, he'd intended to publish the novel with his own imprint, but for various reasons, the business turned out to be a total failure, and so, in the end, his book was brought out in January 2014 by an independent publisher. In the book, Roberto doesn't leave out a single detail of the body of a woman who is brutally pummeled, sliced open, and hung from a sharp metal hook. In the book, he describes with surgical proficiency and coldness the way she's killed and ruthlessly carved in two. In the novel, he doesn't omit the fact that she was pregnant, just as he doesn't omit the fact that she died for nothing. The fact that her death was the result of violence for the sake of violence, that the killer had no motive, only evil. The evil that lay inside the killer.

The author sets forth certain premises and determining factors, if not as motives properly speaking, then certainly as an intellectual explanation of what happened. Roberto Fate makes reference to the treatment of evil by certain authors like Conrad, Camus, Bolaño, Kubin, and Céline. He also touches on an essay collection called *Evil Crossings* by the writer Ricardo Menéndez Salmón, which was published by the University of Oviedo, as well as on *The Aesthetic Justification of Evil in the Young Nietzsche* by Germán A. Meléndez, an academic work published by the National University of Colombia, where Meléndez is associate professor of philosophy. The coldness and emotional detachment with which the narrator treats the facts lend a peculiar style to the work, which nonetheless is not devoid of a certain poetry.

It was Roberto Fate's first published book, and it is striking to behold the coldness with which he describes what destroyed his friend Jacobo. Almost all the events that transpire in the novel are faithful to the incidents that occurred in the Almerían Levant in October 2012. The ill-fated writer Paula Boccia also makes an appearance as a character in the book, although according to his own subsequent testimony, Fate's novel is, in its entirety, a tall tale and piece of nonsense. In the novel, both the killer's and the murdered woman's identities remain anonymous.

Two months after its publication, there was something of a stir, following which the author himself was investigated by the police, but it was amply demonstrated that any involvement he had in the events was entirely tangential, since he was no more than a witness to one part of what happened in Antas, having reconstructed the other part in a work of fiction. Having reconstructed the events of October 2012, in the desert of the Almerían Levant. The events of *the drownings in the desert*:

The first person who drowned in the desert was Elisabeth D., a fifty-two-year-old British woman. She was the second victim of the floods, but the first of the desert drownings. Her body had been dragged by the floodwater to the sea. She was found by a fishing boat about thirty miles south of Pueblo Laguna, the urban center of the town of Vera, where she'd last been seen. Elisabeth D. was an employee of the Vera Beach Hotel, and it was her husband who reported her missing, after which the emergency services and the Civil Guard organized a search effort, until her body was recovered two days later by a Naval Service patrol boat. Of all the deaths, hers had the greatest impact, and a crowded mass was held in the town of Garrucha, where her husband was from.

The fishing boat that first spotted her was captained by

A. Gutiérrez and had cast off from the port of Motril before dawn. While they had decided after all to leave port that morning, the night before, considering the bad weather, they'd decided against it, and Gutiérrez, together with the four fishermen who made up the crew, stopped at a liquor store and bought several bottles of whiskey. Then they all went to the house of one of the crewmen, thirty-four-year-old Esteban Lloret, where they immediately got into drinking and talking about Madrid's latest soccer game, about their families, about women, and finally about the only thing that really mattered to any of them, all except Lloret, who remained silent, guzzling in a corner: the sea.

Lloret, a pensive type with an athletic build, a square jaw, and a crew-cut of coarse black hair, had arrived two years ago from Barcelona, fleeing some murky event, and finding refuge in the home of relatives in Motril, where, despite his last name, his family had originated. He remembered the night's events quite clearly. There was a dream. An alcohol-fueled dream in which his wife's long fingers were caressing his face. He dreamed of her lips kissing his own, kissing his tear-dampened cheeks, and her words, clipped and nervous, telling him they should forget it, that they must put it behind them and think of their life together and their children and nothing else, her words pleading with him to forgive her, begging him to forgive her. Then he remembered falling startled out of his dream, feeling the grip of strong hands moving him, and when he opened his eyes he saw the hawk-like nose, the space between the eyebrows that was populated with long black hairs, the round sunburnt mug of Gutiérrez, who was grabbing him by the shirt and shaking him awake in the dead of night, completely drunk, like the rest of them.

"Lloret, wake up! I saw them! I saw them!" Gutiérrez said, his eyes wide open, popping out of his head with a crazed look, inches from his own.

"What?" he remembered stammering, understanding nothing.

"I saw them! Tons of them!" Gutiérrez went on, shaking him all the while. "There were thousands! Thousands of fish! Fish all over the place, leaping and wriggling, eyes and scales shimmering, right on top of me, all over the place, I was buried in wriggling fish. It wasn't a dream! They were real, they're to the east, to the east of the cape, I know it, I know it . . ." And having said this he stared into the east with a faraway look, as if his eyes could pierce walls and buildings and Cape Sacratif, as if his eyes could see beyond that too, through the storm, through the swell, and through yet another cape, beyond Cabo de Gata, and to the sea near Pueblo Laguna.

Gutiérrez woke everybody up, even kicked one of them awake, and made them leave Lloret's house and slog in the rain to the port. And they cast off, dead drunk, in the dead of night.

They headed eastward under a steady rain. Crazed and sopping wet, Gutiérrez didn't stop talking to himself for a second. A continuous murmuring babble issued from his throat. Surrounded by darkness and soaked to the skin, Lloret thought about what he'd dreamed, about the dream interrupted so brusquely by the crazed Gutiérrez jostling him. Then he thought about his wife. He remembered the time when her parents had spent a few nights in their tiny apartment on the outskirts of Barcelona. It was back in the days when the shadow of a shutdown hung over the factory, those days and nights, that were all one long union meeting. And after one such meeting, when they knew all was lost, when the factory workers knew that almost all of them were as good as in the street, they all went out to get drunk. And he remembered Joaquín, his friend Joaquín, whom he'd grown up with in Badalona, almost like a brother, and who was now a fellow worker in the factory, their lives always running in parallel, welded together, even in misfortune Lloret thought—although at the time he couldn't imagine how much—and he remembered when, drunk and maudlin, he'd hugged him and said:

"And now what, Joaquín? How will I pay for the apartment? How will I pay for the kids' school lunch? What are we going to do?"

And Lloret remembered Joaquín, his eyes also wet, walking him out of the bar and leading him along by the arm, pulling him, almost dragging him through the dark street, lighting one cigarette after another. He remembered how at last they stopped, and Joaquín looked at him and threw away his half-smoked cigarette, and when it looked like he was going to say something, he didn't, and lit another cigarette that again he threw away just after lighting it, and then he told him.

He told him what he'd been doing while Lloret was at the recent meetings, which Joaquín hadn't been going to, with the excuse that he was sick. He told Lloret what he'd been doing with his wife, Lloret's wife, while Lloret and their coworkers were all busy.

Lloret remembered returning home and giving his wife the first of three beatings. While she didn't scream very much, her crying could be heard throughout the house, and he remembered that her parents didn't so much as poke their heads out of their room, and that the following day, after saying goodbye to their daughter and him as if nothing had happened the night before, they were gone.

Over the next several days, he gave his wife two more beatings. He remembered each one of them perfectly. There weren't any others.

And as he was remembering all this, somebody aboard the ship gave a shout, pointing at the dark water. Four and a half nautical miles southeast of Los Escullos, they saw them, and saw her.

They saw thousands of fish, thousands on thousands, and every last one of them dead, and in the middle of all these fish, they saw a woman floating on her back. And while the others stood entranced in the rain contemplating this image, Lloret thought again of his wife, lying still, so still, and also floating, in the sheets crumpled up like a sea or a desert, on their bed in Barcelona, with the purplish mark of his fingers still on her neck, and her mouth open, a gaping hole, *like the silent simulacrum of a scream.*

The second drowning victim was also a woman, Francisca N. J., thirty-four years old, found on the beach by some boys who, for no particular reason, were playing there after the flood. According to the medical examiner, the cause of death was so-called dry drowning, which occurs on rare occasions—only 10 to 20 percent of all drownings—and unlike wet drowning, which is the kind we're all familiar with, when a person starts to swallow water that passes to the respiratory system provoking asphyxia, the cause of this kind of drowning isn't water. The cause of death by dry drowning is a laryngeal spasm leading to prolonged glottic closure, a mechanism whose purpose is to counter ordinary drowning by preventing the passage of water into the lungs, but which, in turn, also prevents the passage of air, leading, in the end, to death by asphyxia. This may give some idea of the colossal, agonizing struggle Francisca endured before dying. Nobody reported her missing. The search for her began only after her three-year-old daughter, wailing incessantly, showing clear signs of starvation, was discovered in her small apartment in one of the poorest areas of the city.

The paradox arises from the first victim of the floods in the Almerían Levant, Joseph V., a ninety-year-old man from Belgium, who didn't die from drowning, but rather from a heart attack as he was being evacuated by a Maritime Safety and Rescue helicopter from the rooftop where he was trapped. He was already a cadaver by the time he was admitted to La Inmaculada Regional Hospital.

The fourth and fifth victims were an elderly married couple who were found in their car, which was completely covered in mud, on La Rambla de Guazamara. Their vehicle had been swept away, quite literally, after they were ambushed by the avalanche of water and mud that buried them alive. They were residents of Cuevas de Almanzora, where they lived with their forty-one-year-old daughter, an only child, who reported them missing. When the policeman who went to break the news to her saw how devastated she was, he warmly gripped her shoulder and said several times that he was very sorry. The woman then seemed to disintegrate even further and broke into sobs in front of the policeman for a few seconds. When she'd managed to pull herself together, she apologized and asked if he wanted a cup of coffee or anything else to drink.

The policeman, even though he was married and had two young children, and despite the terrible circumstances of her parents' deaths, thought the woman wasn't bad-looking, that even though her face was the worse for wear, she was thin and had a good body. So he accepted the offer and went with her into the kitchen, where she turned her back to him as she made the coffee, and he sat down and stared at her ass. For a moment, he felt like a scumbag to want her like this after everything that had happened, but he quickly put the feeling out of his mind. Through her cheap, flimsy dress he could see the outline of her panties and the curve of her buttocks. He thought about trying to fuck her right there, how he'd lift up that housedress she was wearing, pull down her panties, and fuck her. Then, with her back still turned to him, she began to talk:

"Three days ago, the night before my parents left in the car, I dreamed about the sea. I dreamed that, even though we lived far away from it, the sea was rising, creeping over the horizon toward our house. I dreamed I was looking out the window at the other houses that were already being flooded by the sea and collapsing, falling into themselves. I remember running from one window to another, where we saw that the sea was only a hundred feet from the walls of our house. My parents and I rushed to gather up the most valuable things to take with us: coats, money, the few pieces of jewelry my mother kept locked up, photo albums . . . and as I started to look for the videos of my lost son among the photo albums, I woke up. I got out of bed and looked out the window and saw the rain. The never-ending rain.

"It wasn't the first time I'd had that kind of dream," she continued after a pause. "There was one other time when

I had a dream like that, where the sea rises and the houses all fall down. I still remember it, I can't forget it. I can't . . . because the next day my son drowned. It was six years this September since he's been gone. That was the last time I dreamed about the sea, until the other day."

The kettle began to whistle. She took it off the flame and turned around, put two porcelain cups on the table, put the sugar bowl next to them, poured coffee in the cups, and turned around again, her back once more to the policeman, and, looking toward the half-open window, she continued:

"A year after my son's death, my husband and I separated, and I came to live with my parents. Then I lost my job. It's so hard, after working up all the strength you need just to survive, to see the things you scratched and clawed to get in your life keep disappearing, and you know that in the end you're going to lose it all. And now, everything's just like it was in the dream. When I woke up that night, instead of going back to sleep, I just sat on the edge of my bed and waited. I waited for the moment of destruction."

The sixth victim of October 2012 wasn't a drowning, nor, in fact, was the death related to the floods. The sixth victim was a pregnant woman who was brutally murdered, sliced open, and hung from a hook in the semitrailer of a refrigerator truck that was used to ship large slabs of meat.

Beyond a certain point there is no return.
This point has to be reached.

—FRANZ KAFKA

HOUELLEBECQ

1.

When Roberto and Jacobo went to meet Paula, the first thing they saw was what wasn't there, or what was there and yet didn't exist. The first thing they saw was the leg dragging slowly toward them. A leg that wasn't a leg, just a chunk of metal and plastic under the fabric of her pants. Leaning on her cane, she came down two or three steps to exit the bus station, at the bottom of which, she stood before them. Roberto looked at her eyes and she, in turn, for a moment, at his. As soon as he saw them, her dark eyes seemed to him like those of a whale, a giant white whale emerging from a murky, forbidding sea, and then they struck him as the eyes of somebody peering out of another time, of a time that transcends death and holds it always in view, of somebody coming from that time, from a future that was now a memory. It looked just like this:

Then they went to Roberto's apartment and chatted for a while in the living room. Roberto poured them glasses of red wine. Jacobo was friendly and talkative. Roberto, too, but maybe a little more on the pensive side. Only at the end of their conversation did Paula mention anything about her prosthetic leg.

Boccia is a game for crippled people, Roberto thought. And while Paula was responding evasively to Jacobo's questions about her trip, Roberto began to turn this thought over in his mind. He imagined a game, a large game in which they were all pieces moving across a board, a board covered with squares and crisscrossing, entangled streets, like a labyrinth, a game in which arriving at the goal was impossible since everything seemed to indicate that there was no such thing. A game in which the pieces could eat one another, but when this happened it wasn't just the pieces devouring one another but the players who were eating one another, tearing off bloody strips of meat, which they brandished like trophies. Arms and legs ripped clear out of their sockets.

Roberto was jolted out of his daydream by Jacobo, who was excusing himself and saying that he had a previous engagement to attend, but that they'd get together later for a drink and could talk at greater length then.

When they were left alone, Paula and Roberto fell silent. Roberto asked if she felt like another glass of wine. She said yes, she'd take another, and Roberto filled the two glasses. Then, out of the blue, Roberto asked about her manuscript's opening story. He asked about Monkey. Who was Monkey? What was Monkey? Looking him directly in the eye, she began to recite something that Monkey said in the story:

"Once upon a time the pieces fit together, I know, because I've seen them fall apart, in the past, which will be the future, and that memory is. He put the seed in you all, and the seed sprouted in the blood that flowed from violence, and its roots grew strong between the pieces, and these separated and fell. You would like to put them back together, but what's biologically separated can't be put back together by anything at all."

"Yes, that's right . . . ," said Roberto.

"What's broken can't be restored, can't be molded again," she said.

"After that you talk about biology, about the world, about human beings, about the moment we became rational beings, about the conception of good and evil . . ."

"The only things I talk about are parasites and God."

"But that's not God, how could that be God!" he said.

"Yes, it is God."

Then Roberto lapsed back into silence, staring at Paula's serene face and the way her eyes were watching him. He tried to detect weakness and doubt in them, and while there was no hint of these, there was a hint of something else, something that made him look away.

"You know *The Possibility of an Island*?" she asked suddenly.

"Yes."

"Tell me, then, what does a mouse do when he leaves his mouse hole and faces the unfathomable void?"

"Sniffs around."

"That's right," she said. "And every morning, when you get up, open the window, and look outside, you're doing the same thing, and from a certain biological perspective, you're the same subject, and your reaction to the unfathomable void isn't any different: sniffing around. We should just stick to that."

"Yeah," he said, staring at her, and for the first time since they'd met, he dared to let his gaze wander, in front of her, from her face to her body to the form of her body discernible beneath her clothes.

Then, staring at his eyes, which weren't looking back, feeling his gaze on her breasts, Paula asked him what he was reading now.

"I was reading your stories," he said.

"Then what?" she asked.

"Then nothing."

"Nothing?"

"Not a thing," he said.

"So what were you doing?"

"Thinking."

"Thinking of me?"

2.

"To slowly rejoin a maritime death, / We walked across hot, white deserts / And came close to a dangerous abyss . . . / Feline figures were smiling within," Jacobo recited from the book in his hand, sitting in the back seat of Roberto's Peugeot as they drove across the enormous plain cut in two by the highway. To the south, past acres and acres of crops covered in plastic sheets, there was a glimpse of the coastline; to the north, the desert. Paula thought about the passing landscape, she thought about the desert, about the desert and words. The desert and its eerie light, the whole terrain a flood of desolate sun. The arid land was ocher or gray, occasionally reddish, eroded by wind and by rare but always torrential rains that sketched capricious shapes—furrows, cracks, and columns, like sculptures— and hardly anything survived there. She felt overwhelmed by so much beauty.

The damage was still visible from the freak storms that had wreaked havoc in a number of towns, like Vera, Cuevas, and Antas, where they were heading.

Paula had insisted on going with them, against Roberto and Jacobo's advice to stay behind and rest, to attend Michel Houellebecq's poetry reading in Antas. The bizarre territory of the floods was made even more bizarre in the minds of Roberto and Jacobo by the fact that this novelist and poet—notorious for not being much inclined to such events, even in his native country—was going to attend a book presentation and give a reading. The book being launched was a bilingual edition of his poetic work, called *Poesía*, a collection of his four books of poetry, which had just been published in Spain.

Jacobo leafed through the book and then put it in the plastic bag with the other two books they'd brought along to get signed. One was *The Possibility of an Island*, property of Roberto, and the other *The Map and the Territory*, that of his friend. Jacobo thought about this book's protagonist: Jed Martin, a painter and photographer, whose mother had committed suicide and whose father was absent. A solitary man, cut off from the world. Jacobo thought about the remarkable similarity between himself and Jed Martin, and remembered how, in the third part, the novel took an unexpected turn with the appearance of another principal character: a writer called Michel Houellebecq. In this way, the author introduced himself into the narration and, as a character, carried it along toward its gloomy conclusion. The novel's first words were a quote from Charles d'Orléans: *The world is weary of me, and I am weary of it.*

Jacobo also recalled the big scandal in 2011, when the writer's disappearance after the publication of his novel in France provoked a frenzy of speculation. The press began to run articles on the mysterious vanishing act. Jacobo remembered receiving an email from his friend Roberto consisting of the terse sentence: *Michel Houellebecq has disappeared.* He remembered the way these words sunk in, propelling him to look for more information on the internet. The first report in Spanish appeared in the newspaper *La Vanguardia: The writer, whose latest novel, published by Anagrama, was awarded the most prestigious prize in French letters, has changed his telephone number and has not been responding to emails since June. He has not shown up for his book presentations in Amsterdam, The Hague, and Brussels. This has given rise to the most far-fetched speculations concerning his whereabouts. Rumors of all sorts have been circulating online, ranging from a publicity stunt to an al-Qaeda kidnapping, since in the past he has received threats from Islamic fundamentalists. And let us not forget that Houellebecq, with his troublesome and eccentric personality, was interned in a psychiatric unit in the eighties when he suffered an episode of psychotic depression after losing his job. Some years later, in 1994, he would publish his hit debut novel,* Whatever.

Then Jacobo received another strange email from his friend with nothing written in the subject field. When he opened it, he saw three links. Clicking on the first took him to the digital edition of *Le Parisien*, where, despite his limited knowledge of French, he was able to read the following: *The writer Michel Houellebecq, winner of the Prix Goncourt for his novel* Whatever, *has gone missing. He has not appeared at readings that are part of his publicity tour scheduled for numerous cities in the Netherlands and Belgium.* The second and third links took him to the respective websites of *Le Nouvel Observateur* and *Le Monde*, which had also picked up the story.

I had to go to the dentist, but I spent eighteen months there, shut away, writing, without caring too much that my teeth were falling out. Jacobo remembered having read this declaration of Houellebecq's, after the writer resurfaced, offering his apologies. The "there" that he was referring to was his house, at an undisclosed location in the protected region of Cabo de Gata, near San José, in Almería.

3.

When they arrived in Antas, dusk now falling, the first thing they did was go to a pharmacy for painkillers. Paula had explained that she felt frequent pains where the remaining part of her thigh fit into her prosthetic leg. That was why Jacobo had insisted on her sitting up front.

Roberto drove until they found an open pharmacy and parked outside. Pushing his door open, he told Paula to stay in the car and rest, and then he stepped out and stood looking at Jacobo, who made no move at all to get out. Jacobo looked back at him and sensed something cold in his eyes, as if his eyes were frozen in their sockets, frozen or dead, he thought. After a second, Roberto closed the door, and Jacobo watched his friend walk down the sidewalk toward the pharmacy. Then he looked at Paula, who was getting comfortable and stretching out in the seat. He looked at her leg, covered by her jeans. That's where her prosthesis must be, he thought, but the way she was sitting, nobody would ever have imagined that this girl was missing a leg. Then she turned around and looked at him with her big deep dark eyes.

"Hand me the poetry collection, please, Jacobo," she said. After Jacobo handed it to her, she looked at the cover, then opened the book to the first page, where she lingered for a few seconds. Then she flipped through the pages, stopping at random to read a line or two out loud. Her fingers were long and her skin, though slightly tanned, was actually quite fair. She stopped a little more than halfway through the book and read a poem to herself in silence, and then out loud:

> *Teeth crumbling apart*
> *In a gaunt jaw,*
> *The evening turns bitter*
> *And I hit rock bottom.*

> *Amnesia comes back and lasts a few seconds,*
> *In the middle of the crowd time seems frozen*
> *And one no longer feels like fixing the world,*
> *In the middle of the crowd and the mine-embedded paths.*

> *The life, the attempts,*
> *The failure confirmed*
> *I watch the cripples,*
> *And then all is dérive.*

We wanted a prodigious life
Where the bodies would bow like open flowers,
We failed at everything: sad endgame;
I collect the debris with a very nervous hand.

Then she fell silent, and Jacobo looked at her shut mouth. He thought about the act of falling silent, of her speechlessness and what was left hanging in the air after her voice had gone. He watched the way she closed the book and handed it to him with her long fingers, and Jacobo thought of other fingers, long, too, but dark, and wanted to hold them—not Paula's, the other's—to take them and lift them to his lips, hold them in his hands, and he felt he should be elsewhere, holding that other hand, not here, and he wanted to say so, he wanted to say he had to leave, that they should leave, but just then the driver-side door opened and Roberto got in, holding a box of medicine. He handed it to Paula and she said thank you, and Jacobo heard the way she said thank you, and these words, he thought, were somewhere on the margins, on the margins of his life, of his life that wasn't here, that had never been here, of his life that would have to, finally, begin. And he wanted to say all this, but his mind canceled one idea with another—slow down, he thought—and then Roberto said, Let's go, and Jacobo didn't want to say it, but he did, Let's go, and Paula said it too, and Roberto started the car.

Roberto, having asked a man walking a dog for directions to the place where the reading was being held, parked nearby, in front of a bar. Since they had time to spare, they decided to go in and order a few beers. Paula didn't want anything to drink, just a little water to swallow the painkillers. When they were done, they walked slowly, letting Paula set the pace, until they arrived at the ground floor of the post office, where the event would be held.

There were already some people waiting around outside the door and chatting. Jacobo recognized a few professors from the University of Almería and one or two acquaintances from the city. They went in and sat down, talking over Paula's manuscript for a bit while they waited. Roberto had even made a bound copy for the trip, which he'd left in the car. And so they talked about Paula's own stories, and then about the works of Houellebecq, two of whose novels Paula had read: *The Elementary Particles* and *Platform*. There was a point when Jacobo felt a little outside of the conversation, since, when it came to presenting his ideas, he wasn't as sharp as Roberto, whose behavior toward him, moreover, had been somewhat distant ever since Paula had arrived, and so he took the opportunity to go out for a smoke.

The air outside was fresh and unusually humid, as if the threat of rain were still floating in it. Just then, the man of the hour arrived, and when Jacobo saw him, he was struck by his physical frailness. Sporting a brown jacket with white pants and shirt, Michel Houellebecq walked into the room with a man and woman—who Jacobo knew were the philosopher Antonio Muñoz Ballesta and his wife, Nico—to both of whom, as Jacobo was also aware, the writer had dedicated his novel *The Possibility of an Island*. The Frenchman looked much older than his fifty-five years and gave the impression of being sick and beaten, as if his bony shoulders bore the weight of the world.

Jacobo followed them inside and took his seat next to Paula and Roberto in the hushed room, which, despite the

strange circumstances and the sparse publicity, was nearly
full. The presenter and the other guest speakers remarked
on the author's work. When the presentation was over,
Houellebecq picked up a copy of the book and started
flipping through it, as if it were something unfamiliar,
something strange to him. He solemnly began reciting a
poem in French, and when he finished, one of the assistants read the Spanish translation. Otherwise, the silence
of the room was broken only by the applause that followed
each reading. Then the writer began to smoke, and after
that he was never without a cigarette between his fingers
as he made his way through his four books of poetry—
Surviving, The Art of Struggle, The Pursuit of Happiness, and
Rebirth—reciting them in French and then letting one
assistant or another read the Spanish translation.

The last poem that he read was called "Parade":

> *Hanging on your words*
> *I walked at random through the plaza*
> *The skies opened, and I had to play a role*
> *Somewhere.*
>
> *Unfurled, the dead cascade*
> *Spilled fragments of gel*
> *Around my aortic artery,*
> *I felt superficial.*
>
> *Volcano of superfluous words,*
> *Forgetfulness of human relations*
> *A world exists in which people kill themselves,*
> *A world exists among our veins.*

The acquiescence of this world is simple
If one is resigned to lose happiness
The word is not useless,
It comes just before the hour

When the fragments of life explode,
Calmly arranged
At the bottom of a decorated coffin
Frozen velvet, antique wood, old rose.

Velvet like a soft drink
That fizzes skin-deep
Sifted like nomadic flesh
Ripped into thin ribbons

In a universe on parade
A universe where everything is beautiful
In a universe on parade,
In a universe in ribbons.

After the reading, the author gave a book signing. When it was over, Jacobo saw Roberto approach Houellebecq, who was sitting at a table by himself, while everybody around him was chatting. Through the hum of people, Jacobo could make out a few words and phrases exchanged between Roberto and the Frenchman. He heard the word *Camus*, he heard the word *life*, then he heard the word *death*, and the words *writing* and *suicide*, and the word *rose*, and the word *Baudelaire*, and the word *salvation*, and the word *evil*, and then, as clear as day this time, he heard Houellebecq, in his flawed Spanish, say, "No, young man, no, that's going too far," and he raised his hand and, with this gesture, ended the conversation.

They stayed while the room gradually emptied out, leaving only three or four groups of people talking among themselves. Roberto and Jacobo introduced Paula, who was beginning to warm up, to a few of the assistants they knew and they all exchanged opinions about the reading. When they left, they saw that Houellebecq was talking to a tall, curly-haired woman in a black jacket. Each of them was holding a cigarette, and as he stood there shrouded in smoke beside her as if they'd been set on fire, it seemed as though literature and cigarettes had rejuvenated the writer, or at least momentarily reconciled him to the world.

Paula took the initiative and suggested they go have a few beers at the bar from earlier, where the car was parked. The bar was crowded, but there were two or three tables still open. They ordered beer and tapas and sat around the table for a long time, chatting as they threw back one bottle after another. Paula was by now completely at ease and took the lead in the conversation, commenting on various facets of the reading and work of the Frenchman, jumping around to other authors as she did so. Roberto spoke about literature, too, and although he didn't come off as animated as Paula, he responded to all her questions and paid thoughtful attention to what she said. On the other hand, Jacobo, however much he tried to be friendly, found it hard to expand beyond a mere yes or no.

At one point, while Paula, seated between the two of them, was talking almost exclusively to Roberto, telling him something about new South American fiction, Jacobo, who was feeling drunk, sensed her hand touching his under the table. He felt her fingers close around his hand. And her fingers, as if in conflict with her self-assured air, were cold and seemed to be shaking.

After another two beers they ordered some liquor. Whiskey on the rocks for Roberto and Jacobo, and rum and coke for Paula. While they drank, they decided to find a hotel and stay the night in Antas.

They found a small two-star hotel, a wide building only two stories high. They got two rooms, a single for Paula and a double for the men. By now, they were already quite drunk, but Paula was in a boisterous, chatty mood and wanted to have one last nightcap, so they went to the hotel bar only to find it closed, and that they had no choice but to head to their rooms, where, from their adjoining doorways, they said good night. The rooms were clean and decorated simply. There was a heater, which they turned on, and the beds were large, with wrought iron headboards. The few pieces of furniture in the rooms were rustic and made of varnished pine.

Jacobo lay down on the bed, not wanting to get undressed, and closed his eyes for a moment. Opening his eyes with the resolve to wash himself at least a little and take off his clothes, he saw that Roberto had got half undressed and was lying back in bed with his head on the folded pillow, leafing through Paula's manuscript. Jacobo thought for a moment about telling him to take a break, that they would talk about it in the morning, that there was plenty of time, that he was obsessing over the text, but instead he kept his mouth shut, rubbed his eyes, and stood up. He went to the bathroom, where he took off his clothes, turned on the hot water, and got in the shower. He let the water run down his back and felt its warmth. Then he heard Roberto rapping his knuckles against the door and turned off the tap so he could hear.

"Yes?"

"I'm going to Paula's room," Roberto said. And after a pause, "I have to talk with her."

When Jacobo came out of the bathroom, Roberto was no longer in the room. On his bed lay the manuscript of Paula Boccia's stories.

Jacobo lay down naked in bed and pulled the sheet and blanket over himself. He turned off the lamp on the nightstand, and lying there in the dark, he could hear Roberto whispering in the other room. He also heard Paula's voice, but it was muffled and he couldn't make out what she was saying, either, and then, loud and clear, he heard a *no*, which came from Roberto. After that he didn't hear anything else and closed his eyes.

Jacobo closed his eyes, so maybe he dreamed what happened next or maybe it was something he really lived.

One way or another, Jacobo woke up or, still asleep, dreamt he woke up. It was the sound of a smack that woke him. Something smacking violently against something else. Jacobo sat up in the dark—and perhaps in a dream—and looked at the other bed. Roberto wasn't there. Jacobo focused and perked up his ears, but he didn't hear the smack a second time. He pictured something hard hitting something soft, but if that were the case, it wouldn't have sounded the way it had, so he tossed that notion out. It must have been something hard hitting something else hard, something that wouldn't break, and this provided some relief. But the relief was fleeting, so he got up and, neglecting to put on any clothes, went naked into the hallway. He was cold and could feel his body shivering. He concentrated on not shivering, on making it stop, but he couldn't, his body seemed not to be his own. And this body that seemed not to be his own squatted down in front of Paula's door, since it was one of those retrofitted old doors that still have a keyhole, or maybe it wasn't, maybe it was that way only to explain how Jacobo could see through the door into Paula's room. So he saw through. The lights in the room were on, and through the door he could see the bed, and on top of it Paula, naked with her legs open, that is, her one leg and her stump open, showing her vulva. She had a big bush of pubic hair that was gray and entirely covered her groin, but as Paula slid her fingers into herself and spread herself open, forming a darkness in the middle of that gray, the hair shifted and fell off, like something weightless, and Jacobo realized that it wasn't hair, it was ash. It was gray ash that falling away, revealed a pink sex. Jacobo looked at it and then looked at Paula's face and her eyes, whose dark centers began to roll back, and back, until they disappeared, leaving nothing but white. Her eyes now two blanks, she turned until she was in profile at the edge of the bed, and then her body began to shake just as Jacobo sensed there was another presence in the room. Her body arched back, it arched so much it looked as if her spine would snap, and then the presence manifested itself. Roberto appeared. He was naked and his erect member was enormous, red, and covered in veins that looked as if they were about to pop. Roberto went over to Paula and penetrated her with his gigantic organ, making her wriggle like an animal. He grabbed her hips and yanked her against him, thrusting harder and harder. And Jacobo had the feeling that it wasn't Roberto who was entering Paula but she who was entering him, or rather, was being consumed by him, as if Roberto were a black hole, and Jacobo saw Paula's skin begin to turn white, and then translucent, and he heard her moaning as her veins and capillaries grew visible beneath her skin, which had become as thin and transparent as tracing paper. Then, with a roar and a final thrust, Roberto apparently came. And when he took his member out of her, it was covered in blood, which dripped into a spreading stain on the floor, and Jacobo was certain, without knowing why, that the blood came from Roberto and not from her, and was certain, too, that she'd become pregnant, and then he heard a buzzing, and only after hearing it did he see them, he saw the bees swarming around Paula, hundreds of bees, flying around her in concentric circles, and he fixed his gaze on her sex and the blood flowing from it, and he had the feeling that it was pollen that was red and dark.

4.

Jacobo looked out over the beach under the last light of day. He found it disturbing, as if everything were corrupted, sadly corrupted. Large storm clouds were gathering in the sky, and in the pale, fleeting last light, he saw the beach as a woman, a woman who was still young, who has had wishes, hopes in a life, in what she thinks of as a full life, a woman who has searched, too, as part of this fullness, for love. She's searched for it time and again in different men, and met only with disappointment, and then sadness and lack of affection, and only once, fleetingly, as fleeting as the foam from the surf that recedes and disappears, love and sadness, a deep, wide sadness. This woman, thought Jacobo, this beach, was foul, corrupted, defiled by men. There was a greenish debris of plastic and glass, and far at sea one could still make out a dark smudge that might have been a school of fish, but deep down he knew it wasn't.

Then Jacobo looked at Abeba and saw in her profiled face the same traces of filth, of disappointment, but they weren't obvious yet, they were no more than subtle hints imprinted on her skin, on the tissues joined to her facial muscles, on her grimace, on the way her jaw *hung* from her face, but that wasn't the word, he thought, that was not the right word. Then he thought of Roberto, he thought of that night after the reading, he thought of Roberto's contorted face, he thought of his vision, what he'd seen in Paula's room, he thought of Roberto's enormous, unreal member, and he thought of Paula, of Paula sitting at the foot of his bed when he woke up:

Her big black eyes were patiently watching him when he opened his own eyes to find hers in his view. At first he felt confused, but in a way he wasn't surprised that Paula was there, dressed for the day, her perfectly groomed hair falling long and black around her shoulders. Then he looked over at Roberto's bed, and she, following his eyes, explained:

"I made his bed while you were sleeping, not that it needed it, but I just did it while I was waiting for you to wake up. It's an old habit and old habits die hard. Roberto's waiting for us in the café."

Her use of the plural, which included him in some kind of unit along with herself, bothered him, but to a certain degree he knew it was how things were, that they were joined by something they perhaps sensed and that, in turn, they were each a part of, something each one of them longed to discover but also feared to discover, something that Roberto seemed to have already found. Something Roberto had found that had changed him forever.

Jacobo propped himself up in bed and noticed that Paula, still sitting down, wasn't wearing shoes, her one foot rested on the cold floor next to what substituted for her second foot. He stayed where he was for a few seconds, waiting for her to get up, but she didn't look like she intended to. He was wearing only underwear and felt ashamed of her seeing his flawed body, but he swept the blanket and sheet aside anyway and sat for a moment on the bed before he stood up. He planted his feet on the floor. He could feel the heat drain out of his body and into the floor as his feet turned cold. He looked at Paula's only foot, sure that it must be freezing, like the floor. He thought that it was like an attitude toward the world, toward life, choosing another option, that was all. Then he tried to understand why he'd thought this, tried to understand how this might be an attitude toward anything, but the notion had escaped his mind, flown far away, and he let it go. He got up, and his paunch hovered at Paula's eye-level: his navel, the center of his body, he thought to himself. He went to the shower, leaving the bathroom door ajar, there was no longer any need to close it, not anymore, he reasoned. He pulled down his underwear and felt a pang of dread when he saw blood on his genitals. He looked for a wound, but didn't find anything. Then he got in the shower and let the hot water wash away the dried blood. He checked himself again—not even a scratch. The red-tinted water streamed over his legs and disappeared down the drain.

When he came out of the bathroom, Paula wasn't in the room. He hadn't heard her leave but he supposed the sound of the shower had drowned out her footsteps. He got dressed, packed what few things he'd brought into a duffel bag, and left the room. Paula and Roberto were at the front desk. He saw them before they saw him. They were talking in low voices, their faces very close together, both looking deadly serious. When they saw him they suddenly stopped talking and exchanged a look as if they didn't recognize each other, as if they'd just woken from a dream, and then they looked at him like that, in the same way. Until Roberto said: "Let's go." They left and headed to the car.

It was already late in the morning, and the sun shone as if it had never rained, as if no water had ever descended on everything, sweeping away and destroying in seconds whatever lay in its path.

They got on the highway and, for more than half an hour, drove in silence. Then, without saying anything, Roberto took an exit and headed down a service road. Jacobo, who was in the back seat, noticed Paula look at Roberto in surprise, but she didn't say anything. Neither did he. After a few miles on the service road that ran parallel to the highway, Roberto turned right, onto a narrow, paved lane.

"What are we going down here for?" Paula finally asked.

Roberto didn't answer, but Jacobo saw that his friend's jaw was clenched, and noticed that his fingers were gripping the steering wheel tighter. Then, in answer to a question that nobody had asked, he said:

"I have to stop for a minute."

He pulled the car off the local road and onto a plot of land that appeared to be of hardened clay but from which a fine cloud of dust rose when the car stopped. Roberto got out of the car without saying anything and walked into the sparse scrub that covered the esplanade. They watched him disappear behind a low embankment.

First it was Paula who got out of the car and then Jacobo, but he soon caught up with her. Paula took Jacobo by the arm, leaning on him as they made their way down the dirt embankment. Roberto was up ahead, sitting on top of a mound of rocks with his back to them. From where they were standing, it looked like Roberto was staring at the horizon, but when they got closer, they saw that his eyes were glued to the ground's reddish dirt. His eyes were also red.

Paula went over and bent down beside him. Jacobo, standing at a short distance, thought at first that she was kissing him on the cheek, but then he realized that she was whispering something in his ear. All of a sudden, Roberto got up, spun around, and shoved Paula, who fell backward onto the ground. Jacobo was frozen to the spot by the sight of his friend's face, twisted into a grimace—of rage, he thought, or pain or disgust or all these mixed together.

"It's a lie!" Roberto yelled.

"It's all a lie!" he yelled.

On the ground, Paula clutched where her stump fit into her prosthetic leg and choked back a cry of pain. Standing over her, Roberto began talking, slower now, and softer. His voice didn't seem to come from his throat, but from further inside, much further, as if he were talking to himself from within himself, from a gloomy, obscure inner space:

"There's only one world. And it's a false, cruel, miserable world, where there's nothing but pain, pain and atrocity, cruelty and atrocity. A world where there's no such thing as meaning, where there's no way, where there's no goal. I want to live, I need to deny this world, this world where we're not still mere evolutionary machines, where we try to understand, to account for the pain that's all around. Everything begins with pain. Everything ends with pain. Reality isn't a whole, it's a part that's dismembered, mutilated, and connected by pain," he said, with a faraway look, staring off at something that neither Paula nor Jacobo could see.

Jacobo was still frozen in place, his eyes fixed on his friend, while Paula cradled her stump in both hands, her face covered in tears and dirt. Suddenly, Roberto screamed: "Pain is God!" And then he lowered his voice again, until it was almost a whisper: "We fool ourselves, we need the lie to declare false victory over what is real. The entire edifice of culture is a farce, a necessary lie we weave to escape, to prolong the agony. Art, literature, they're just the negation of *the truth*. *The truth*," he repeated, "the pain that connects everything, even a body that's destroyed, dismembered but alive, but made one by pain," he said, and nudged Paula's prosthetic leg with his foot. She moaned in pain on the ground, tensing her facial muscles.

Then Roberto yelled again, even louder than before, as if he'd gone out of his mind:

"There's no salvation! Literature won't save us! Don't you get it? And you're a piece of shit . . . A passive piece of fucking shit . . . Why don't you do something? Why don't you say something? Say something!"

And as he yelled this, he delivered a brutal kick to Paula's prosthetic leg, ripping it from its fastenings.

REBIRTH

When they left the beach and got back on the highway to Murcia, the first drops that had started falling soon turned into a rainstorm. As if everything were happening the way it had before the floods had come, or as if they had never receded, but had somehow remained latent like a threat. The road was barely visible, the rain formed a curtain and seemed to worsen by the second. As he drove, Jacobo thought about what had happened that day and the days before. He felt far away from all that now. Abeba held her stomach and stirred, too, restlessly, in the passenger seat.

They had to go away, start over, erase everything that had happened before, they had to save themselves, thought Jacobo. He had to save himself and save her, this dark-skinned woman who now felt somehow joined to him, he had to save her from the death he foresaw in his dreams, which now, after everything that had happened, he sensed to be quite real. Then he thought of Paula writhing in pain on the dusty ground, and of Roberto staring idiotically at the plastic-and-metal leg lying in the dirt, as if it were part of a doll that some kid had ruthlessly ripped to shreds. Meanwhile, *the doll* writhed in pain and grabbed at air, as if trying to hold onto the leg that wasn't there anymore.

Jacobo remembered himself fleeing that gruesome scene. He remembered Roberto's words, words that seemed to be spoken by somebody very different from his friend, but that he understood were very much his own. His own because they came from inside him, from the deepest part of him.

Jacobo saw himself fleeing, escaping from that shot in which Paula's body squirmed on the ground and Roberto stared hypnotized at the leg lying several yards off, static on the earth, as if attracted to it by some irresistible force.

A leg like the tail of a wall lizard.

A tail that doesn't move.

While the body of the lizard writhes.

Then he saw himself again, getting into Roberto's car and starting the motor and hesitating for a few seconds over what to do next, while the motor hummed, and finally putting it into first gear and taking the narrow, paved road to the highway, and then heading to Almería.

Only nine hours had gone by, but it all seemed so distant, so unreal, Jacobo thought. The escape in Roberto's car, arriving in Almería and desperately looking for Abeba, finding her and asking her to leave with him, for somewhere else, anywhere, as long as it was far away. Then his mind came back to the present moment, to the place they were in, to the ceaseless rain, to Abeba beside him in the passenger seat, moving her hand toward him, her long, dark-skinned hand that touched the fair skin of his cheek, and without being able to help it, like the rain, the falling drops can't help it, a tear trickled down the white skin and onto that other dark skin.

The rain grew stronger until it was almost useless to

look out the windshield. He saw a sign for a rest stop up ahead and decided to take the next exit. He merged onto the service road and drove a couple miles until he found the entrance to the rest stop, which was an enormous, paved esplanade with trees along its fringes, where numerous eighteen-wheelers were parked. At the back, there was a hotel and off to one side of it there was a café. Only after he'd parked the car in a covered parking area with a metal roof did he realize that this place must be very near where he'd abandoned Paula and Roberto. He tried to not think about it, to make the thought disappear from his mind. He glanced at Abeba, she looked tired, and her eyes were swollen. He brought his hand to her cheek and caressed it. She took Jacobo's hand, in turn, and pressed it harder against her face. Jacobo noticed that Abeba's temperature was running high and that she was shivering.

"Wait here," he said. "You shouldn't get wet. I'm going to check out the café and bring you something hot."

When he took his hand from Abeba's face, she said something to him in a hushed voice, something he didn't understand. He looked at her but didn't ask what she'd said, and got out of the car.

He walked quickly across the lot, trying not to get too wet, though it seemed the rain was slowly abating. He passed several refrigerator trucks, walking in the darkness of the shadows cast by their trailers. Half the lamps were broken, and he lost his bearings, until he saw, behind a truck, the lit entrance of the café. The place was empty inside, except for a man around fifty years old doing something behind the bar. He went up to the man. He was wearing a white shirt. Jacobo ordered a coffee and asked for another two in plastic cups to go. The man said he didn't have plastic cups, and that he'd have to drink the coffee there. In the end, Jacobo got the man to pour the coffees into an empty plastic bottle. He also bought a couple sandwiches.

When he left the café, there were only a few drops of rain coming down. He hurried back through the parked trucks to the car and, turning the corner around the back of a truck, he found himself face-to-face with him. The face staring at him with its wet eyes looked disfigured. But I left them, I left them in the desert, Jacobo thought, but then he realized that it was indeed possible, that he'd come here on foot. Jacobo uttered the name of the person whose face it was. The face answered him in a whisper, saying something Jacobo could barely hear, then saying it again, and Jacobo, who heard it clearly the second time, said *my God*, then he noticed the stone in the hand, the hand at the end of that arm, that arm that was joined to that body to which clung soaking clothes, and he saw the face, and all Jacobo could do was say *my God* again, and nothing more—he felt a hard blow land on his head, and everything went dark.

When he came to, the first thing he noticed was the cloying taste of blood in his mouth, then he felt the hard asphalt beneath him. He sat up and touched his head. The cut on his temple didn't feel too deep. He was cold and wet, but he didn't care. The only thing he cared about was finding Abeba as fast as possible. He didn't know if he'd been unconscious for five minutes or an hour, it was impossible to tell. He got up and went to where he remembered parking.

When he got to the car, the passenger-side door was open and Abeba wasn't there. He was overcome by absolute terror. He walked a few yards into the parking lot, softly calling for her, whispering her name as if he were afraid of being heard because he understood now that he was capable of anything. He went out from under the metal roof and walked alongside a large refrigerator truck. Turning the corner around the trailer, he was surprised to find that the cargo doors were open. As he was about to walk past, he looked inside the trailer, and there, just within the light of a streetlamp, he saw her, and was confronted with the most horrific sight a human being can observe.

From the roof of the trailer, on a hook used to transport large slabs of meat, hung the body of Abeba cut open down the middle. The hook pierced her throat and lower jaw, suspending her a few inches above the floor. And as Jacobo looked down at the floor, taking his eyes off that vision, he saw the blood gushing from her halved body, from her entrails, from her dead unborn son, as if the blood were being reborn, and falling to the floor of the trailer and trickling outside, toward his feet. And on the parking lot asphalt, an enormous red rose was forming, its petals opening, growing larger and larger, an incredible red rose, expanding as if it held the bloodshed of all the mutilated innocent, all the innocent who were dismembered without understanding what was happening to them, who were beheaded and tortured as they looked on with uncomprehending eyes, while they wondered why, from all the desecrated innocent, from all the children, women, and men annihilated by terror, by the terror of the twentieth century, by the terror of the twenty-first century, all the blood that will be shed by the terror of the twenty-second century, by the terror of the human being. A horrible, huge, beautiful, endless rose.

CPSIA information can be obtained
at www.ICGtesting.com
Printed in the USA
JSHW031201191122
33480JS00004B/24